MW00676193

Murder at the Panionic Games

Murder at the Panionic Games

Published in 2002 by
Academy Chicago Publishers
363 W. Erie Street
Chicago, Illinois 60610

Printed and bound in the U.S.A.

Library of Congress Cataloging-in-Publication Data

Edwards, Michael B.
Murder at the Panionic Games / Michael B. Edwards.
p. cm.
ISBN 0-89733-500-7
1. Greece—History—To 146 B.C.—Fiction. 2. Athletes—Fiction. 3. Priests—Fiction. I. Title.

PS3605.D89 M87 2002
813'.6—dc21 2001053482

DEDICATED TO
MY WIFE, SYLVIA,
AND
MY DAUGHTER, KATHERINE,
WHO GOT ME STARTED.

CHAPTER I

I COULD HEAR THE MURDERER'S footsteps as he entered the sacred cave. He took no particular care to be quiet. The slap of his sandal was distinctive against the bare rock of the cave floor, and it echoed back into the enclosure where I stood waiting. I knew that he could not see me yet, having entered from the bright daylight outside into the cave's murky gloom. Even when lit by dozens of smoking oil lamps perched on small ledges, the cavern was gray and shadowy at best. Now that I had extinguished all the lamps but two or three, the darkness was heavy and cloying.

His stertorous breathing grated on my ears as he peered into the depths of the cave, attempting to distinguish me from the various statues and pieces of furniture that sprouted from the floor like overgrown mushrooms every few paces. I sat silently almost at the very back of the deep hole, watching him carefully with the desperate hope that my trap was going to work. I could see from his outline next to the statue of the god Poseidon against the brightness of the entrance that he held a short sword in his right hand, and swished it impatiently through the air at his side, to and fro, to and fro. I had a sword also, my father's old family relic, sleeping quietly in my lap, but I knew I was no match for his prowess with the weapon. If it came to a fight, it was quite likely that this would be the one and only mystery I would ever have the blessing of Poseidon Helikonios to solve.

"Bias!" he barked sharply. "I know you are in there. Come forward and speak to me."

I remained silent and sat as quietly as a shocked virgin bride being introduced to her new husband for the first time. He swung his head back and forth, his eyes trying to pierce the darkness. I was about a fifth of a stade from him in the depths of the cavern, say forty paces. Unless he came into the cave after me, there was no chance he could see me. He took a few hesitant steps forward and stopped again to peer within.

"Bias," he called again. "That was a challenge you issued last night. You knew I would be here. Come out where I can see you, man, instead of skulking like a damned Carian in this hole. Come out!"

Still I sat quiet as the tomb, which uncomfortably reminded me of what this sacred enclosure could become if I was wrong in my estimation of the murderer's personality and his need to brag of his deeds. I really had no hard proof at all that he was the killer, and unless he confessed it himself, the city magistrates would never believe me over him. His position was virtually unassailable by only a minor priest of the Panionic altar and sacred cave of Poseidon Helikonios.

He was growing frustrated, the short sword swinging more fiercely now. He edged further into the mouth of the cavern and paused beside a statue of a nymph, his free hand resting against her bare ribcage. He would be able to spot me as soon as his eyes adjusted to the gloom, and I needed him further inside the hole. My hand slippery with the sweat of fear, I lifted my slow, old sword and scraped it against the bronze incense stand next to my chair. He froze, and his ears seemed to prick up. He lifted his head, almost like a dog sniffing the wind, and smiled.

"Yes, I knew you would be here," he called softly. "The gods will not help you now, little priest. Your life has run its course, and this is the end of the race. You might as well accept your fate and come out. I promise you that I will end it quickly and you will not have to suffer. That is a greater reward than many men receive at the end of their lives." He shuffled a few more paces closer.

"I am not coming out, guestslayer," I announced in what I hoped was a bold tone. "But you may come in, and be punished by Poseidon!" He looked startled at the noise, and then grinned wolfishly. Sweeping his long tunic back from his sword arm, he started forward, and I rose to meet him.

❋

This charade of death began five days before, at the beginning of the great festival of the Panionia. If you had asked me then, I certainly never would have guessed that the celebration would turn out like this. I had worked for the entire spring month of Thargelion under the sharp eye of the major priest, Crystheus, in preparing the sacred grounds of the Panionion for the festival and the great athletic games. Athletes and spectators from all twelve cities of the Ionic League would be flocking to the festival, the greatest of all the impressive celebrations of this part of the Greek world, and Crystheus was absolutely determined that no criticism whatsoever, large or small, could be laid at his hearth, concerning the cleanliness or state of repair of the religious grounds. And even though he was only two years older than I, his status as the major priest and mine as the minor, ensured that he was the supervisor and I, the lowly laborer.

One day around the middle of the month, about ten days before the arrival of the first competitors and celebrants, I dashed the sweat from my eyes and protested halfheartedly to him that the work would go much faster if he could see his way to descend from his pedestal and assist me in some of the heavier labors, such as the repair of the west wall of the Altar Hill, in which I was presently engaged. He smiled, oh, so patiently, at my scowling countenance.

"Bias, Bias, Bias," he murmured, staring at me fixedly. That was another of the many things that I disliked heartily about him, his habit of repeating words and phrases over and over.

"Bias, Bias, Bias. You are well aware that your duties as the minor priest of Poseidon Helikonios include the physical work that is necessary to keep these grounds in perfect order. The outer beauty of our site here is the reflection of the inner perfection of our service to the protecting deity of our home city, yes, our home city of Priene." Caught in the asinine drama of his pronouncement, he swung an arm about him at the rocky grounds upon which I toiled.

The Panionion, the religious and political meeting place of the twelve cities of the Ionic League, covered several acres on the north slope of Mount Mycale, a long, spiny ridge that separated the site from the city in charge of its management, my "home city of Priene."

To our north, about three stades away, say six hundred paces, the Bay of Samos and the blue waters of the Aegean

Sea gleamed in the spring sunlight. Mount Mycale wrapped around behind us like the inside of an archer's bow, with the west end of the bow running like a knife blade along the peninsula that points toward the island of Samos, and the opposite side of the bow projecting northeast toward the Maeander River valley and the great non-Ionian Greek city of Magnesia-on-the-Maeander. If you trek about twenty stades over the top of the ridge to the southeast, you will come to the city of Priene, the most beautiful, if not the most powerful, city of the league, and its harbor town of Naulochus, which stands guard on the northern side of the bay where the mighty Maeander empties into the Aegean. On the southern side of that same bay towers the greatest city of the entire Greek world, magnificent Miletus, whose dozens of colonies and far-reaching trade surpasses even that of legendary Athens.

The Panionion itself consists of the great altar, a sacred cave sinking into the guts of Mount Mycale to the southwest, and the Panionic bouletarion at the bottom of the ridge below the cave.

The altar of Poseidon Helikonios and its surrounding walls are the most difficult structures for me to keep in good repair, as they are out in the open and subject to the whims of Aeolus, the wind god, who takes great pleasure in covering the marble altar floor with dirt from the plain before us. The altar itself is large, about twenty paces by six, and let me tell you, many a bellowing bull has met its glorious end on its shining marble slabs. In fact, it is considered good luck if the sacrificial victim bellows during the ceremony. Mind you, I believe this is just an old wives' tale.

The altar is surrounded on all sides by gray ashlar walls of a tall man's height, being three stone courses from bottom to top. Straggling along these walls both inside and out are flower beds of colorful asphodels and anemones, which are the very deuce to keep healthy and blooming with the breath of Aeolus constantly in their faces on one side and being shadowed by the cursed wall on the other. The whole structure is entered through an arched entrance halfway along the west wall. If you stand on top of that arch and look to the west, you can barely see the green island of Samos beyond the tip of the peninsula about eighty stades away.

Seventy paces to the southwest of the Altar Hill is the sacred cave. Various statues of minor gods and goddesses adorn its interior, which is dominated by the large statue of the Lord Poseidon just inside the entrance. There are several marble chairs and tables, and copper incense burners scattered about upon the leveled rock floor. I have always thought that it smelled musty inside the sacred cave, which, upon reflection, is not so unusual, since the entire shrine is dedicated to Poseidon Helikonios, the god of the sea and the earthshaker.

Below the cave at the foot of the ridge is the bouletarion, where the delegates from the league meet to thrash out various common problems. It crouches there like a half-completed theater with eleven semi-circular rows of seats and a diameter of about forty paces. However, instead of a stage, there is only the levelled rock, and where the side entrances would normally be are transverse blocks of stone. It is open to the front, facing the bay to the north, and in the middle is a speaker's dais of marble.

This, then, was my kingdom and my responsibility, or rather, my responsibility under the guidance of the good Crystheus, who at that moment had ended his dramatic gesture and was lecturing to me again.

"Oh, yes, Bias," he pontificated, "visitors from all of Ionia will stop here to worship and ask for the blessing of Poseidon on the great games, and we must insure that nothing intrudes upon their consciousness that would hint of ugliness or even mediocrity."

I sighed in exasperation, and again wiped the sweat from my forehead.

"Crystheus, what does that have to do with your helping me with these flower beds and stone walls?"

He gazed at me benignly through his protruding eyes.

"Bias, the point is this. How can I accomplish the myriad tasks assigned to the position of major priest if I utilize my time doing the work of the minor priest? How can you hope to become the major priest when my term is complete if you do not master the tasks, yes, the tasks assigned to you now?" He gestured vaguely toward the cave and the bouletarion.

"What myriad tasks are you referring to, oh major one?" I protested, looking about in feigned consternation. "There are no suppliants here to pander to, and it is already mid-day."

"Mid-day, mid-day!" he exclaimed in his squeaky voice. "Gods, you are right, my Bias. I must be off to Priene, and speak to the cattle merchant Eusthavius about the bullocks needed for the sacrifices on the opening day of the festival."

Whirling away in a swath of snow-white wool chiton, he added over his shoulder, "Do try to finish that last stone of the west wall today, Bias, and then begin on the north wall."

My mood was sour as I watched him stride jerkily down the hill, and then up toward the path that led over Mount Mycale to the city. Plopping myself down on the top of the offending block of stone, which had some boy's graffiti scribbled on it in charcoal, I turned my gaze to the south and watched the sunlight bounce off the sparkling cool waters of the Aegean. A swim would certainly go down well right now. With a gusty sign, I considered my position for the hundredth time.

I am, as you have without doubt surmised by now, the second of two priests of the Panionion. In order to serve in this position, one must simply be a young man of good family from the city of Priene. These qualifications, I am happy to say, fit me admirably. Being born in this sunny port city on the banks of the Maeander twenty-three summers ago and being an outwardly staunch believer in the powers of the Lord Poseidon, I am amply qualified to be the minor priest. Indeed, I believe I am amply qualified to be the major priest, but the city fathers of Priene unfortunately considered Crystheus more prepared than I. These two positions are filled by the magistrates every three years, and although nobody can point to my family as being less than honorable, neither do they compare it with Crystheus' family, who supposedly are descendants of the one and only Aepytus, a grandson of Codrus, the last king of Athens. Yes, *the* Aepytus, who founded the city of Priene during the initial Ionian migrations two hundred years ago. It is difficult to try and compete on an equal basis with the descendant of *the* City Father.

At any rate, the securing of the position of minor priest six months ago was a great boon to me and my large and hungry family. While my forebears are as aristocratic as the next man's, his purse may be somewhat greater than mine and his family somewhat smaller. The minor priest of the Panionion receives a handsome stipend, though obviously not as handsome as that of the major priest. It is very annoying that Crystheus does not need the stipend at all. His family is one of the larger landowners of the city-state of Priene. This line of thinking brought me back to my original thought, which is why he got the job in the first place. I sighed again.

Traditionally, the minor priest serves his three-year term and then is appointed by the magistrates as the major priest. This had not happened in Crystheus' case, however, because the last minor priest had died after being gored by a maddened boar in a hunting expedition just before assuming his higher post. Subsequently, Crystheus was appointed without any prior training and no effort at all, while my father had labored mightily to obtain the minor priest position for me. At the bottom of the issue was the hope that I would graduate to the better job in thirty months or so. Of course, when I got the sinecure, I did not realize that my duties would include all the physical work to be done at the site. There are two leaders and no followers at this location, so it is not difficult to see how I ended up as the sole follower, or donkey, if you will.

Realistically, I must admit to myself that I am fortunate to have the position at all.

I love my father, Holicius, very much, but the gods do not, and I find it hard to make up for their indifference with even my mightiest endeavors. He has not been able to prosper in farming, which is necessary to keep up one's station here. Our small estate lies along the southern slope of Mount Mycale to the west of Priene rather than in the rich Maeander River valley to the east, due to my great-grandfather's late arrival from mainland Greece as a settler in this area. My father's Herculean, but mostly futile efforts, kept our family together and fed, but that is about the most that can be claimed. I suppose my childhood might be described as that of a young scion of the genteel poor.

Unfortunately, my father was very good indeed at another endeavor. That is the production of a large and hungry family of females, with only one male to balance the load: me. Five years after my own arrival, at intervals of every eighteen months or so, my mother, Tesessa, bore my father a new daughter. They finally finished attempting to produce another son when six daughters were on the scene. Thank the gods, all these girls were born perfectly healthy and remained thus, so that our family was something of an oddity with all children surviving. On the other hand, the resources of my father's small estate have been strained to the utmost in keeping all of us healthy and relatively happy in our situation, and with the oldest girls now at marriage age, the producing of dowries becomes an increasingly gloomy, dark cloud on the horizon. As I have said, our bloodline is as good as almost any in Priene, but in this modern age, bloodline does not go far when not pushed along by appropriate talents of gold and silver.

My stipend as the minor priest has helped the situation a good deal. While it does not place me in the same league as King Gyges of Lydia in his golden citadel, it does enable me to help build those dowries so necessary for my sisters' welfare. Indeed, my oldest sister, Ulania, who was eighteen last month, has been betrothed to a third son of a former city magistrate, and with any luck, they will be married in the month of Boedromion in the autumn. I realize that is a late age for marriage, but better late than never. Indeed, if you had seen this aristocratic third son with his nonexistent chin and crossed eyes, you would be amazed that his father could capture any girl at all for him. But money talks, and he is not demanding too high a dowry. My father leaped upon the match like a starving man presented with a dish of peacock's eggs.

My father's next task, then, will be to find an eligible bachelor for my second sister, Arlana. This may be even more daunting than finding Ulania's darling, since Ulania is pretty in a mousey way, while Arlana has a wraithlike figure, sharp facial features that remind one of a ferret, and a tongue sharper than her features. Indeed, Arlana can flay a man to ribbons with that tongue in a matter of moments. She does not suffer fools gladly—I know because I have been on the receiving end of that razor-like appendage on numerous occasions. With this combination of body, face, and personality, you can see why my father has begun taking nervous, if calculating, sideways glances at Arlana when we are sitting as a family. However, even that harmless occupation has earned him scornful ripostes from her, father or not. Arlana is not an advocate of parental respect, though I am quite confident that this attitude will reverse itself when, and if, please the gods, she ever becomes a mother herself.

The other four girls are not a problem at this time, being too young for marriage now. Risalla, plump and rosy, is fourteen years old. Tirah, brown and spritelike, is twelve. Tapho, merry and carefree, is the next at ten, and the youngest at eight is Elissa, golden and beautiful as a miniature goddess, my father's special delight. I, the sole son to be considered, am not a problem either, since males frequently do not wed until their late twenties.

As for my looks, they should neither help nor hinder my marriage prospects. When I glance into a glass, a pleasant young man stares back at me, of medium height, with lanky, dark brown hair worn slightly shorter than fashionable shoulder length. Nothing to catch the eye, so to speak, but nothing to make a beautiful woman shudder either.

With a last long sigh, I reluctantly turned back to my task of cleaning this portion of the west wall, scrubbing and scraping at the offending lines of charcoal graffiti. Curse the boy who writes on my walls, I thought morosely, although the sentiment was not far from the truth, declaring "Crystheus is an old maiden aunt."

This last bit of doggerel expunged, I spent the next several hours weeding and watering the flower bed along the inner portion of the west wall. There is a trickle of spring water from the rocks in the northwest corner of the Panionian property that provides us with all the fresh water we need. Lugging it from the spring to the small hill in leather buckets was pleasantly mind-numbing, and allowed me to let my thoughts wander over the hills and valleys of the domain of Priene and even across the blue bay to the islands of Samos or Chios, the westernmost reaches of the Ionic League.

With the inner west wall free of protruding weeds and pithy sayings, I noted that the sun was about a hands breadth above the horizon in the same direction. In an hour the god Helios would have finished his mad dash across the sky in his chariot of the sun, and be relaxing at Mount Olympus, the home of the gods, after a hard day's work. I reflected that this was obviously what I, the servant of Poseidon, should do as well, though my family's farm was hardly Olympian. With this comforting thought in mind, I stored away my gardening tools and buckets, and started up the slope to cross the rocky top of Mount Mycale, heading for home.

CHAPTER II

THE ATHLETES, SUPPORTERS, spectators, and moneymakers began to arrive in Priene a week before the beginning of the Panionian festival. They flooded in from all parts of Ionia by the hundreds, each arriving for a different reason, with disparate dreams and hopes, and by every imaginable conveyance under Helios.

From mighty Miletus and tiny Myus they came, and from the great city-state of Colophon, where the horse ruled supreme. The artists of Lebedos and the painted Lydia-lovers of Clazomenae arrived. The people of Teos, venturing out of their houses of blue limestone, were there, and the competitors from Erythrae, where the river god Axus is worshipped. The mariners of Chios and Samos, where the temple of Hera is one of the marvels of the Greek world, swaggered in to Priene's port of Naulochus, swearing and spitting. From Phocaea came the athletes who abide by the word of their harbor's seals, and from the wondrous city-state of Ephesus arrived the followers of the many-breasted, strange goddess Artemis.

They came on foot, by chariot or by cart, from cockleshell boats and strong oared ships, and on horseback, donkeyback, or any other back they could manage. The merchants, traders, musicians, artists, and slaves quickly filled the inns to bursting, and communities of brightly-colored tents sprang up along the various twisting roads leading into Priene and Naulochus. Of course, the aristocrats and all the athletes were welcomed into the city homes and outlying estates of Priene's wealthy landowners, but even these spacious buildings were soon straining at the seams.

The Panionion festival with its great games only happens once every four years. Although not quite as magnificent as the tremendous Olympic games in mainland Greece across the Aegean Sea, there is no contest to equal it in all of the lands under the sway of the Ionic League cities.

It would begin, of course, as did all major festivals, with a procession through the narrow streets of Priene with beautiful young women and handsome local men of good families leading the beasts that would be sacrificed at the Panionion shrine. Following the fortunate (or unfortunate, depending on how you look at it) animals, which were to be dedicated to the gods, would stride the great athletes of the cities of the League, all eager to compete in the physical contests that would bring glory to their cities and fame to themselves. Then would come the musicians and poets from near and far, just as ready as the athletes to compete for lesser honors and riches.

The actual procession would commence on the morning of the first day of the festival, and so naturally, all who were there to participate or watch and enjoy, arrived beforehand in order to be able to gain accommodations, visit old friends, conduct business, commit minor crimes, and indulge in the hundred and one activities available to large crowds of people in small places. As they arrived and Priene filled up, bursting from within and spreading up and down the coast between itself and its port, I continued to prepare the Panionion grounds for the initial sacrifices and religious programs that were scheduled to occur.

All the enclosing walls of the hilltop altar were sanded and scrubbed down, until not a single carved graffiti word could be noted. I swept the altar floor at least once a day and repaired the southeast corner, where the top block of projecting marble had been chipped by some clumsy worshipper or by a recalcitrant gift to the gods with sharp hooves or horns. All the statues of the gods in the sacred cave had to be washed, repainted, and generally made ready for admiration, and the cave floor swept and leveled, so that enthusiastic visitors would not trip and brain themselves while oohing and ahhing over the likeness of Poseidon or his wife, Amphitrite. I carried in fresh rushes to cover the floor and renewed the olive oil of the many lamps along the cave walls. Although it was unlikely that the League Council representatives would meet during the festival itself, I also descended onto the bouletarion council structure like a cousin of Aeolus and cleaned it from its cobwebby wooden top to its dusty marble bottom, until the seats gleamed in the morning light. The wildflowers that I transplanted around the sacred grounds from the nooks and crannies of Mount Mycale danced violet, red, yellow, and white in the breezes that continually swirled about the small hill, cave entrance, and council building.

In other words, I slaved like a barbarian, while my erstwhile senior priest companion enjoyed the leisured business activities of his office. Since we Greeks believed that a gentleman should not have to demean himself in hard physical work, except athletics, I clearly had some way to climb in order to reach this plateau of social acceptance.

Nevertheless, as I dragged my weary frame home toward my father's farm on the afternoon before the day the festival began, I had to admit that the place looked well-organized. If the city magistrates found anything lacking in the preparation of the Panionic shrine, it would not be due to a lack of effort on the part of yours truly.

As I have mentioned, our estate is located to the west of Priene. It is nestled in a small stream valley between the city and the port of Naulochus, but at a slightly higher elevation. Priene itself crouches at the mouth of the Maeander River, and thus is in a perfect position to control the trade routes that extend east into the kingdom of Lydia and use the river as their outlet to the Aegean Sea. Priene's merchant vessels, while not anywhere near the status of the ships of Miletus, Samos, or Chios, nonetheless are numerous and keep us well supplied through Naulochus with the goods that make greater Greece the envy of the known world. Confidentially, it is with the blessing of the gods that we have our port city, since the River Maeander is so rich with soil swept downstream from the great farmlands of Lydia, that Priene is already experiencing difficulty in remaining on the Aegean coast, as the coast keeps desiring to move westward while the river mouth silts up! Some learned sophists have even predicted that in 200 years Priene will be land-locked and some stades from the edge of the bay, but I believe this is carrying science a little too far. Still, I suppose one should not scoff at what one knows little about.

In any event my father's land is up far enough on the slope of Mount Mycale above the main road, that the tent cities of the festival visitors had not stretched up onto our land. However, by this time the tents extended nearly all the way from the city to the port, and the din and bustle was incredible. There seemed to be every imaginable type of person, animal, cart, and tent at hand, and not just places for the visitors to live in, either. In order to provide the visitors with food, drink, and all other kinds of goods, colorful merchant stalls had sprung up everywhere.

I strode past hawkeyed traders of all sorts, bawling out their offerings of water and wine to quench your thirst; lamb, mutton, and goat for hungry mouths; herbs and incense to sweeten stifling tent interiors; and tunics, chitons, and cloaks to replace clothing that had become frayed or dirtied during the traveler's journey to the mouth of the Maeander. For the ladies, there were brightly colored robes and hair ribbons; knitted sakkos for those who liked to sweep their hair upward into a netted roll; and numerous examples of the jeweler's art, from rings and ear baubles to necklaces and long, old-fashioned chiton securing pins.

I paused at one stall to drink a kylix of weak wine and water, poured clear and sparkling from a heavy psykter. The tubby, sweating merchant was from Miletus across the bay, he claimed proudly, and was making a killing at this festival. I eyed him narrowly, but refrained from any cutting remarks, as his wine was pleasant and refreshing and I was in a tired and peaceful mood. Flipping him a half-stater coin, I thanked him for the drink and strolled further down the road to where the dirt track branched off to the right, climbing gently up the slope of the pine-covered ridge toward my father's and several other miniscule estates. Here at the small crossroads was an untidy cluster of temporary dwelling places, constructed of pieces of wood, awnings, animal skins, and rope. Several small children were running about with cheerful shrieks, and on a chair in front of one tent lounged an oikema woman, who smiled lazily and waggled her fingers in the age-old manner.

"Come, my handsome one, and step into my little cubicle. You look like you are tense and could use some relaxation. My rates are very reasonable."

I considered her offer for a moment, but knowing the penurious state of my purse, I shook my head regretfully and continued up the dirt path toward the small estates. She hooted behind me.

The boundaries of my father's farm began about a stade up the dirt path on the left. As you turned off onto a branching path, the native trees and bushes immediately gave way to an olive grove with the respectful and thoughtful olive trees standing in rows that guarded either side of the path. The grove covered a good three acres and was my father's main source of income, since olives and olive oil are the basic food staples of the entire Ionian world. Further up the slope toward the house was an acre of green and healthy grapevines, growing avidly in the spring sunshine with the promise of hundreds of bunches of wine grapes for the fall. Although the best wine in Ionia came from Chios, we could afford that only for the most special occasions, and therefore made do with our own local vintage. In a good year my father even had enough to sell to winemakers in the city, thus earning a few extra silver talents to help the family finances.

When harvesting time approached, my father, I, and the family's two male slaves girded up our loins and toiled manfully in either the olive groves or the vineyards from sunup to sundown. Again, this was not the way that an Ionian gentleman was supposed to live, but hunger and thirst compel one to do things not always consistent with one's desired social status.

The house popped into view ahead of me as I rounded a corner above the vineyard, and strode thankfully up onto the porchlike prodomus. Although it was only late spring, Helios's chariot of the sun was beating down ferociously, promising a long, hot summer. With any luck the grape crop would be an excellent one this year, allowing my father to add some talents to my sister Arlana's dowry in order to tempt the unwary into overlooking her sharp tongue.

Our house was built in the standard fashion of a small country estate—that is, it was two stories high with the covered prodomus lurching out of the front to welcome visitors, a small three-storied defensive tower hooked to the right side like an afterthought, and a miniscule courtyard in the back, surrounded by a man-high wall that attempted to proclaim that the family of Holicius observed all the proprieties. The walls were of sun-dried mud brick strengthened by timbers, the entire structure resting on a strong stone foundation. Not an imposing edifice by any means, but a staunch, plain house, where three generations of my family had grown up. With only minor repairs now and then, it still squatted as solidly as it had seventy-five years ago, when it was built by my great-grandfather.

At this time of day, I knew the family would be relaxing in the courtyard, so I strolled through the main corridor leading directly to the rear of the house. At another time of the day, my father might be in the andron room at the front, entertaining, socializing and discussing farming and philosophy with visiting neighbors, and my mother and sisters in their gynaikonitis rooms, spinning or weaving or doing all the many things that really made a plain house into a pleasant home. In the late afternoon, however, we normally gathered in the courtyard, where my sisters tended the family flower garden under my mother's sharp eye.

"No, no, no, it will not do," my father was protesting fussily, as I walked through the back door into the courtyard. "It will not do at all!"

My mother, Tesessa, frowned at my father in exasperation, and glanced over at my sisters, Arlana and Risalla. The former's sharp features were set in a glare of disdain, and the latter's rosy, round face looked about to burst into tears.

"Good evening, all," I chirped cheerfully, and was immediately engulfed in the dirty hands and laughing faces of young girls, as my sisters, Tirah, Tapho, and Elissa, converged upon me from three corners of the garden and flung themselves on me in welcoming abandon. Who needs children of your own, I reflected happily, when little sisters worship at the altar of your feet.

Disentangling myself momentarily, I kissed my mother on her smooth, proffered cheek and embraced my father, who by now was glowering at Tesessa.

"The girls are quite old enough to participate in the festival's opening procession," my mother said patiently. "Indeed, this is an appropriate way to have Arlana noticed by a fine young man of marriageable age." Arlana shot her a withering look, but kept her thoughts to herself for the present.

"But the procession is getting out of hand," Holicius replied. "The last one ended up with three girls romping in the bushes with 'fine young men.' It was the scandal of the city. Surely you don't want your daughters subjected to that!"

"They won't be subjected to that if you and Bias are constantly on hand. You know as well as I do that those girls were not properly attended, and that is what happens when men or women get too caught up in these modern ideas of freedom and irresponsibility."

"That's true enough, I suppose. But showing off one's daughter is not the way to get her betrothed. I must seek out our old neighbors and make arrangements for Arlana's future with one of their young sons. It is just not correct to have her 'noticed' at a procession."

My father's last statement was apparently more than Arlana could bear, and she rounded on him furiously. Peering through Elissa's golden curls, as I held her on my lap, I contentedly thanked the gods—not for the first time—that I was a brother and not a father.

"I have no desire to be 'noticed' by any *man*," Arlana cried, her voice thick with scorn, particularly on the word 'man.' "Flaunting your body in that disgusting procession is for lesser women, not for me!" I considered quipping that she did not have much of a body to flaunt, but wisely kept my witticism to myself.

"Oh, no," wailed Risalla, who at fourteen years of age, was quite prepared to flaunt her robust body whenever possible. "I want to march in the procession! It's not fair that I should not be blessed by Poseidon just because Arlana doesn't want a man!"

Arlana whirled to face Risalla. "And what do you know about men, you little piglet? The only men you've ever met are Father, our slaves, and our *illustrious* brother!" Her verbal arrow bounced harmlessly off my thick hide, and I smiled innocently at her.

Risalla jumped to her feet, and flung herself on my father, nearly knocking him over. "Father, don't let her speak to me like that! Please, please, please let me march in the procession. I want to help pour the wine for the athletes! Please, please!"

Holicius was slightly built, and not much taller than his rapidly growing third daughter. He certainly did not weigh as much. Seeing that he appeared to be having a hard time standing upright with Risalla wound about him, I rose to my feet, unpeeled her like a vine from a trellis, and gave her a gentle shove away from him.

"Go help your sister in the kitchen," I suggested to her tear-streaked face. I could see my eldest sister Ulania squinting out from the kitchen door. Risalla flounced over to the kitchen, set apart from the house in the left side of the courtyard wall, to aid in the preparation of the dorpon meal with Ulania and our one female slave, Selcra.

"Thank you, my son." Holicius carefully readjusted his chiton and sat down again on his wooden bench. He turned back to Arlana.

"Although your assessment of the procession is not very respectful, I agree with your desire not to march in it," he intoned to her pompously. "I will make proper arrangements for a husband for you when the time is right, not because some rogue meets you in the street."

"You will make no arrangements for me, father," Arlana spat at him. "I will never let a man take me, unless it is one whom I can control!" With this retort, she grabbed Tirah with one hand and Tapho with the other, and stamped off to the far side of the courtyard to dig energetically at some offending weeds in the flower bed. My mother looked calmly at my father, and bestowed a serene smile on him. Both she and I knew that he would almost certainly give in to Risalla and let her march in the procession, but would make it seem like his idea. The gods only knew what Arlana would do. My father sighed, and turned to me.

"So all the religious grounds are in readiness for tomorrow's opening, my son?" he inquired. Holicius' firm conviction was that since he had procured the position of minor priest for me, his overall supervision was needed to ensure that I did a proper job. Also, this was obviously an excellent way to steer the topic of conversation away from Arlana.

"Yes, Father," I answered. "Everything is cleaned up, swept down, and shipshape. I have no doubt that the magistrates will be duly pleased with both the condition of the grounds and the arrangements Crystheus and I have made for tomorrow morning. I'm confident that Poseidon Helikonios is already satisfied with our hard work."

Holicius glanced at me dubiously to make sure that I was not speaking flippantly of the city's major deity, continued to smooth out nonexistent wrinkles from the folds of his chiton, and went on.

"When I was in the city this morning, magistrate Euphemius told me that all the official delegations of the other league cities have arrived safely. I look forward to speaking with the delegates again." He plucked importantly at his beard. My father did not know more than a half-dozen men from the other league cities, but liked to believe that he himself was well-known and sought out every four years when the Panionic Games were held in Priene. Certainly a harmless affectation, and one that made him happy.

Our female slave, Selcra, brought my father and me kylixes of wine mixed with water, and indicated that the dorpon would be served soon to us on the dining couches or klines in the andron. Holicius preferred to observe the proprieties in the evening, so he and I, as the family males, would dine reclining on klines in the front of the house, while my mother and sisters ate in the gynaikonitis at the rear of the house. For the ariston meal at sunrise and the deipnon meal at midday, we were not so formal, and the family ate as a group, with my mother presiding over the whole affair.

"I understand the procession is to begin two hours after sunrise?" Tesessa inquired gently.

"Yes, Mother," I smiled back at her. "That should give us plenty of time to get to the city to see it if we leave shortly after dawn." In Ionia the days are divided into twelve equal segments of daylight and twelve equal segments of darkness, so that day and night hours are not the same except on the two equinoxes of the year. Since we were now in late spring, the daylight hours were longer than the night hours, giving us a little more time to walk to the city in the morning.

"I'll make sure the girls go to bed early tonight, then," my mother mused, and fondly took my hand, as I sat next to her on her bench.

CHAPTER III

"OH, HERE THEY COME, here they come!" squealed Tapho and Tirah in harmony, as they spotted the leading girls of the procession pop from around an outcrop of black rock up the side of Mount Mycale. "Where is Risalla, where is Risalla?"

"Hush, now!" admonished my mother. "She's a little farther back. You'll see her in a moment." My three youngest sisters bounced up and down from excitement, waiting for Risalla to appear, so that they could shriek with pride. My mother and eldest sister, Ulania, held tightly onto them, so that they would not bolt out into the procession path. Arlana, of course, had refused to attend at all.

The procession had begun at the outskirts of Priene on the other side of the ridge, had proceeded up and over the mountain like a giant snake slithering over a big log, and was descending down the slope as if pouring from a hole behind the craggy rocks. In order to get a decent view of all the participants, people had lined the way all along the entire route with most of the onlookers either at the beginning of the parade near the city or with us at the end near the Panionion. I was standing with my family about two stades up from the altar hill, waiting to signal Crystheus that the marchers were in sight, so that he could begin final preparations for the ritual sacrifices.

The leading girls, chosen for their pretty faces, admirable figures, and their fathers' heavy purses, were now coming down the ridge face. Each was to act as spondophorai at the ceremony, so they lugged a jug or bowl for the libations of wine at the sacrifices or for slaking the athletes' thirst further along in the parade. They sported their best linen chitons in a variety of colors, the predominant being different shades of purple. The chitons were ankle-length, pinned along arms and bodies with small bronze brooches and cinched in the middle by either a linen or leather belt. Since they were young and unmarried, their shining hair cascaded to their shoulders and was adorned with combs and baubles of all descriptions. Some had their faces whitened with powdered lead, but again, being young, many wore no makeup at all, and you could see the rosy flush on their cheeks and necks. Thoroughly delightful, I must admit.

"Risalla, Risalla!" screamed my sisters, pointing and jumping. They had spied our family marcher coming down the dusty hill now, and could not contain their enthusiasm. People watching beside us shot approving side glances at them, as it is no mean thing to have a family member in the Panionic procession. Risalla's normally rosy complexion was deeper than usual, and she beamed a satisfied smile on all the observers as she passed. I noticed that she had pulled the hem of her chiton up a few inches as she had flounced along, so that it swung at mid-calf, showing off a bit of her strong, plump legs. My father also noticed, and his proud smile turned down a bit at the corners at this minor breach of etiquette.

"Father," I said nudging him slightly in the ribs, "I must report to Crystheus, so that he will be ready for the sacrificial animals." He nodded, distracted, his worried eyes on his daughters. I headed down the ridge through the throngs of people toward the altar.

Crystheus did not need much warning. He had one of our temporary helpers perched on top of the surrounding wall, shading his eyes and peering off into the distance, watching out for the head of the procession. This young worthy recognized the first girls with their wine jugs at the same time I reached the enclosure, and bawled down to the major priest that the column was in sight.

"You were supposed to warn me, yes, warn me of the procession's arrival," snapped Crystheus at me, as I hurried in through the gate.

"Plenty of time, noble Crystheus," I soothed, as I drew to his side. "I made sure everything was prepared ahead of time. All you need to do is meet the procession at the altar wall gate, and I will give you the materials for the sacrifices."

His protruding eyes considered me doubtfully, but he hurried over to the gate, where he could just spy the first girls in the distance through the crowd. They hurried along the track toward us, dancing to and fro, chitons swirling, eyes sparkling, and laughter pealing through the air. Behind them we could now see the young men of the city, who had been designated to lead the sacrificial beasts to the holy grounds. They were coaxing and pulling several small male oxen, all of beige color, because the god Poseidon Helikonios preferred light-colored offerings. Next came several more boys dragging unwilling white nanny goats to be used to appease Poseidon's mate, Amphitrite, after the god had been satisfied. As is the way with goats, their capering and leaping was making much more of a spectacle than the oxen, who plodded along in serenity, unknowing and uncaring.

The onlooking people were chattering and waving wildly by now, pointing out procession participants they knew and calling to one another in pleased recognition. Some religious festival processions are somber and quiet, as might befit a celebration of one of the gods of the underworld, but this was not one of them. Poseidon was a boisterous, loud god, rightly called The Earthshaker, and the Panionic games procession was always clamorous and exciting.

Now, coming into view after the animals, were the reasons for the games themselves—the athletes from all over the Ionic League. The crowd's buzz erupted into deafening cheers and yells as the staunch young hopefuls from twelve city-states strode proudly into sight. On came the burly wrestlers, the muscular boxers, and the lithe foot-racers. Waving and grinning at the crowds were the horse racers, the discus throwers and the javelin hurlers. All wore short tunics to display their fine physiques, their muscles rippling and bunching in the sunshine, as they displayed themselves to the envious throng. These athletes had much to hope for—by excelling over his peers in the games, the successful athlete gained great honor. By competing he risked not only his own reputation, but also that of his kinsmen and fellow citizens. In addition, he could expect to receive generous material goods upon his return to his native city-state. I have to admit, I cheered as enthusiastically as any as they approached the walls, until Crystheus snapped at me to attend to my duties.

Finally, bringing up the rear of the parade were the artists, who had flocked into Priene for the other aspects of the festival, the poetry, music, and drama contests. While the newest local compositions were offered at the festival of Laneon in the winter, the Panionic games drew artistic participants from the entire Asiatic Greek world, so it was an opportunity to view the most renowned works performed by the greatest actors, poets, dramatists, and musicians in all of Ionia.

Clustered by the altar wall gate and talking quietly among themselves in a tight knot waited the city magistrates of Priene. Their smug expressions showed that they were pleased with the proceedings up to this point, and they occasionally pointed or gestured towards the girls, animals, or athletes heading our way. Behind them on several tables stood row after row of wine psykters, amphoras, and kylixes made of black and red pottery for use by the major priest and the athletes. A quick glance completed my final check of the materials on the altar table to insure that none of the necessary instruments had stolen away on little feet, and I turned back to the gate just as the girls arrived. Like multicolored chicks, they took their prearranged places at the side of the group of magistrates.

The young men then led the animals into the enclosed area, tugging and swearing under their breath as the goats, aroused by the excitement of the crowd, were energetically trying to break free. Even the three stolid oxen were growing restive now, rolling fearful eyes and pawing at the hard ground. I signalled the small group of auletes off to the side to commence playing their religious music. They laid to it with a will, startling Crystheus, who was trying to look solemn, but was only succeeding in looking pompous. He shot me another sour look, to which I returned a calm smile.

Having filled their bowls and jugs from the amphoras on the tables, the girls were pouring the watered wine into kylixes held out by the magistrates, who were then handing them gravely one by one to the athletes, some of whom accepted their kylix with due solemnity, while others grinned and bobbed. I recognized a few of the more well-known sportsmen, including Priene's own hopefuls, Tyrestes and Endemion, both of whom were trying their best to keep from breaking into grins and just barely succeeding. They were our two best candidates, and I had watched them compete in several local events during the past six months. Personally, I thought Tyrestes was the stronger athlete, particularly in foot racing, but either of them might have a chance for glory and honor at the right day and time.

"Bring him up, bring him up!" Crystheus snapped impatiently at one of the young men hanging onto a recalcitrant ox, and the youth began dragging it forward toward the middle of the altar. As the animal handler approached, I held a large bowl of water out toward the major priest, who ritually washed his hands with a few waving motions, and then sprinkled some of the water on the suspicious beast, who snorted and eyed him balefully. I thought it would be a good touch for the crowd if the ox bellowed for good luck, but a snort was the most he was apparently willing to give us. Crystheus then gestured the crowd to silence, waited for the chattering to die down, and portentously pronounced his prayer, while simultaneously tossing handfuls of unground barleycorn at the victim, the altar, and various participants.

"Oh, great Poseidon, Earthshaker, Lord of the Sea, and Protector of Priene and these holy grounds, hear my plea," he intoned, stretching his arms toward the statue of the god standing expectantly at the entrance of the sacred cave. "Accept this sacrifice and the others to follow as indications of our respect, fealty, and devotion. Bless this festival and these games with your favor and goodwill. Smile upon our city and the competitors here today, and turn away your wrath at our unintentional lapses in your worship!"

With this Crystheus motioned vigorously for his designated mageiros to approach the increasingly nervous ox. He had chosen one of his many cousins as this sacrificer, and I glanced dubiously at him, hoping this slight young man had the strength to fell the ox with one blow. The cousin cautiously sidled up to the animal, determinedly licked his lips, gripped his large axe in both hands, and swung a prodigious chop, simultaneously muttering a short incantation. At this point the ox, who by now had had enough of the whole affair, chose to swing his head sharply against his young holder, who was jolted backwards several steps. The axe descended, neatly sheared off the ox's left ear, and clanged off the marble floor. The small wounded bullock roared out his disapproval, and proceeded to knock the mageiros to the altar floor, where he bounced quite satisfactorily several times in a rearwards direction. The infuriated ox advanced precipitously several steps towards Crystheus, who promptly screamed and tried to claw his way out of harm's sight. Only the gods know what would have happened next if I had not scooped up the axe, shouldered aside the shouting major priest, and dispatched the beast forthwith with a sound blow to the head. The poor animal collapsed, kicking furiously on the altar floor and spraying blood in all directions.

Crystheus stood as still as the statue of Poseidon, staring at the dead ox, while the shouts of dismay and bad luck from the crowd grew in volume.

"By the gods,' I hissed at him, thrusting the sacrificial knife into his hand, "get on with it to calm the people!" He blinked several times, drew a shaky breath, and crouched down to cut the bullock's throat. I caught the gush of oxblood in a wide bowl and theatrically splashed it about the middle of the altar as Crystheus struggled to regain his composure. In the meantime several of our helpers rushed forward to gut the ox, place his innards on a small pyre off to the side, and torch the pyre, offering these parts of the animal to Poseidon. It took a few moments, but the pyre had been liberally doused with oil and flared up, consuming the substantial offering as the smell of burnt meat wafted about the enclosure. The crowd, still muttering, stared at the sacrifice and at the surrounding rocky ridge, expecting perhaps to see some tangible evidence of Poseidon the Earthshaker's wrath. When nothing apparently was going to happen, the noise and foreboding started to recede like the tide going out, and relieved sighs and chuckles could be heard. I glanced over at the magistrates, who had ceased to peer apprehensively at the people around them and were acting more at ease.

The remainder of the sacrifices were conducted with no signs of displeasure on the part of Poseidon or Amphitrite, and none of the other animals made the slightest disturbance when led to their doom. Crystheus did himself credit by pulling off the rest of the ceremony without a flaw, drawing exclamations of admiration from the throng as he deftly wielded his sacrificial knife amid prayers and showers of barleycorn on all concerned.

The final part of the ritual was now to be performed. The major priest received a kylix of wine from one of the waiting magistrates, and the athletes drew in closer to the altar, their kylixes raised high in salute to Poseidon. Crystheus ceremoniously poured some of his wine on the burning pyre, causing it to hiss like a disturbed snake and produce a cloud of smouldering smoke. He raised his kylix in a completing salute, lowered it slowly to his lips, and drank deep, scanning the athletes' faces as he swallowed. The expectant gymnasts enthusiastically drained their own cups, and then turned and held them on high to show the waiting spectators. The crowd burst into clamorous cheers, saluting and calling to the competitors from their home cities.

The raucous cheering continued for several minutes, while the athletes basked in the glow from the admiring throng. I motioned for the helpers to start setting up the braziers to begin roasting the sacrificial feast for the procession marchers, when from the corner of my eye, I noticed our own Tyrestes pass a shaky hand over a pale face slick with sweat, then clutch his belly with an agonized moan! I took a stride toward him, and he suddenly staggered several steps to his right, grabbing at a startled Endemion for support. Tyrestes slid to the ground, the other athlete trying vainly to hold him up, and vomited violently onto Endemion's sandals.

I and two other competitors close by reached the retching athlete, just as Endemion lowered him to the dirt. Tyrestes stared wildly at his fellow gladiator from Priene for an instant, gurgled deep in his throat, tried to rise and collapsed, his hands clawing the air. I thrust my fingers deeply against his neck to feel for a heartbeat, found none, and looked up in stunned silence, feeling the gorge rising in my own throat. The other athletes around me involuntarily took two or three steps hurriedly backward, thrusting their hands out in supplication to Poseidon as pandemonium erupted inside the walled enclosure.

CHAPTER IV

"He was poisoned," lisped the iatros calmly to the roomful of listeners, who hung on his every word. "It is quite evident."

"What was it?" inquired the magistrate Valato in a near whisper, peering wide-eyed at the healer.

"A common enough drug," sniffed the iatros, a tall, stately man. "It is called melampodium or hellebore. Very useful as a medicine in small amounts, but a deadly poison when administered in a large quantity." He glanced condescendingly about the andron, as if daring his listeners to question him, and hoping they would, so he could drawl out another learned answer.

We were gathered at the estate of the magistrate Nolarion, which happened to be the closest appropriate house to the religious grounds at the Panionion. After the crowds had disbursed, grumbling and murmuring, to their various permanent or temporary homes, servants had transported the body of Tyrestes by litter to Nolarion's house, to await the arrival of his family. They would claim the body and take it back for proper preparation and burial. It had not been easy persuading the throngs at the Panionion to give up their gawking and prophesying and go home; they were sure they had seen a clear foreshadowing of the young athlete's death in the bungled sacrifice of the first bullock. Everybody knew that the efficacy of a sacrifice was dependent upon meticulous observance of closely defined rules. The ritual must have the right words spoken and the right actions performed at just the right moment. Since this had obviously not been the case in this morning's activities, there was ample reason to believe that Poseidon Helikonios had demonstrated his displeasure by striking down one of the competitors from his home city.

Other than the litter bearers, only Endemion and I had physically touched the slain athlete. This was important, since those people closely associated with the dead were considered polluted, particularly those who had physical contact with a corpse. I did not look forward to being set apart from everybody, and forced by custom to wear black clothing and cut my hair. I did not even know the man! At least, I would not be expected to tear at my own flesh or utter loud (and usually pretended) lamentations at his passing. The others at the site, including the magistrates and Tyrestes' fellow athletes, had been noticeably careful not to touch the body after he had collapsed onto the ground.

"How is the poison administered?" asked Nolarion solemnly of the physician, who looked pleased at the question.

"It can be taken in either food or drink. Although somewhat bitter and dry to the taste, this could be disguised by a strong-flavored stew, soup, or wine. It works fairly quickly in large doses, and by Tyrestes' reactions, reported by Bias here, I would say he had ingested it only a short while before."

"So you are saying this could not have been an accident?" asked the third magistrate, Euphemius, hoping that the healer would contradict him.

"Oh, no, of course not." The iatros waved his hand. "This was a large amount of the drug—much more than a medicinal dose. Unless Tyrestes himself was taking the drug, which does not seem likely considering his physical prowess and superb condition, somebody else would have to have administered it to him." The men in the andron glanced at each other speculatively.

"This . . . somebody," ventured Valato. "It would have to be a person familiar with medicine?"

"If you think that only a physician has access to the drug, then I must disappoint you," said the iatros dryly. "It can be obtained by anyone with enough money to pay." Valato did indeed look crestfallen at this pronouncement.

"Thank you. You may go now." Nolarion ordered the healer. "Please accept my thanks for your swift response to my request for your attendance."

"Certainly, magistrate." The iatros smiled indulgently, as he let himself quietly out of the room, escorted by one of Nolarion's several body attendants.

I let my gaze wander over the various people in the room, with a belated wish that I was not one of them. On the three klines against the three walls of the room away from the entrance door were the magistrates, Nolarion, Valato, and Euphemius. These were the most powerful governmental executives in the city-state of Priene at this time, having been elected by a majority of the city council for a one-year term each. Priene proudly boasted a democratic, as opposed to an oligarchic, monarchic, or tyrannical form of government. The free citizens of the city-state, which included all landowners and their adult sons, were part of the assembly, which met occasionally to discuss weighty matters pertaining to Priene's future. The council, consisting of twenty members of the assembly selected by lot, prepared business for the assembly to discuss. The three magistrates were the executive officers of the government, serving without pay, and basically running the day-to-day workings of Priene in between council and assembly meetings. I studied each of them in turn, as they talked quietly among themselves.

Nolarion was the wealthiest of the three, having the largest and most fertile estate. His lands on the very banks of the Maeander produced an impressive amount of grain and figs, and the size of his sheep and goat herds equalled those of any two other assembly members combined. Nolarion was a large man, just beginning to turn from muscle to fat, even though it was evident he tried hard to keep the physique that had made him one of Priene's most famous athletes twenty years before. His magnificent thick black beard curled halfway down his broad chest, and he tended to stroke it with gentle fingers as he spoke. About forty-five years of age, he had been a magistrate off and on for a dozen years, highly respected and admired.

Valato was almost his physical opposite, being birdlike and timid. His appearance, I knew, was deceptive, as I had observed him speak many times at the council and the assembly, of which my father and I were both members. He had a powerful, booming voice, which easily reached every corner of the impressive Priene bouletarion, surprising everyone who did not know him. How, they would ask themselves, could such an impressive voice come forth from such an unimpressive chest? At any rate, it did, and he had the temper of a bantam rooster to accompany the surprising voice. His well-trained sophistry cut many an opponent to figurative ribbons on the bouletarion floor, and once he had an opponent in his grasp, he would not let up, but would shake the subject to death, as a terrier shakes a rat. His bald head gleamed and his short light brown beard bobbed as he spoke earnestly in the soft evening light. Like Nolarion, he had served several terms as magistrate.

Euphemius physically struck a note somewhere in the middle between these other two disparate government officials. This was his first term of office, and he appeared to defer to his more experienced colleagues. I knew that he had a large estate near the port of Naulochus, and invested the majority of his wealth in grapes and olives. His groves produced the finest oil this side of the Aegean, it was said, and his wine nearly rivalled that of Chios. He was very tall, tended to stoop as he walked, and possessed a stiff iron-gray beard that flowed almost to his convex belly. His clothes were very fine linen of the palest white, and he looked vaguely like a giant stork, as he bobbed about. Not a very impressive speaker, I was told, but with a mind like a dagger's edge. Just goes to show that you cannot always tell by looking at someone.

In addition to the three magistrates in the andron were myself, Crystheus, and Endemion. I was here since I was the last to touch Tyrestes alive, and Crystheus, of course, was present because the death occurred on the grounds of his tiny kingdom. Endemion had two claims for his presence. Like me, he had held Tyrestes in the dying competitor's last moments of life, and in addition, was the eldest son of Nolarion, in whose house we all currently debated.

Nolarion cleared his throat thoughtfully after the departure of the physician and cast a dubious eye at us all.

"It appears, then, if we can believe Martosius, the iatros," he began cautiously, "that unless Tyrestes took his own life, he was, uh, dispatched by somebody else." All of us responded to this statement with appropriate humms and hahs.

"I simply cannot believe this has happened in our city. Are you implying that Tyrestes was murdered?" demanded Valato softly, his fingers drumming on the edge of his wine kylix. We considered this question, turning it around in our minds like children inspecting a new ball, until Euphemius spoke.

"It is quite obvious that he was murdered. We are talking about the best athlete in Priene, set to compete for the greatest honors in all of Ionia. Can anybody in his right mind suggest that such a man would take his own life?"

"But murder," murmured Crystheus sadly. "This just cannot be true, not on the grounds of the Panionion. It just cannot be!" We regarded him solemnly. He was voicing the hidden thought that all of us harbored—that the miasma or pollution created by a murder, especially on sacred ground, would endanger the festival, the games, the city, and indeed, any citizen's house that the killer was received into, however unwittingly. It was almost like an insidious fog or mist that could creep on catlike feet down the city streets, infecting all the people it touched. Crystheus wrung his pudgy hands, and peered at all of us in turn imploringly. Prudently, I did not open my mouth.

"Very well, then," ventured Valato, clearing his throat, "let us assume that Tyrestes was murdered. Martosius said that the poison must have been introduced into his body by food or drink taken not very long before he collapsed. How could this have been accomplished?"

Endemion spoke for the first time. "All the athletes, including myself, were given wine to drink in a libation to Poseidon Helikonios at the ceremony. Is that not correct, Father?" He directed his question to Nolarion, who was staring at him unblinking.

"Yes, my son." The big aristocrat answered slowly, flexing and unflexing his huge hands. "But those drinks were given to all of you by us, the magistrates. Are you saying that one of us destroyed the best chance that Priene has to win the Panionic games?"

The incredible foolishness of this thought struck us all simultaneously. The Panionic festival and its attendant games were the most important internal event in the entire political and social structure of the Ionic League. It was one of the few bonds that held together the tenuous philosophy of what an Ionic Greek was supposed to be. There are not very many of these bonds, you know. We Greeks tend to be a very independent sort of people, and cling tenaciously to our small city-states.

We excused Endemion's next outburst, attributing it to his relative youth.

"I am as good an athlete as Tyrestes," he exclaimed heatedly, flinging his arms wide as if casting an imaginary fishing net. "I can equal him in most of the events of the pentathlon! I will win for Priene!" As soon as the words left his mouth, Endemion realized what he had said, and reared back in deep embarrassment.

"Forgive me!" he choked out, and stumbled to his feet from his chair. "I did not mean to denigrate his abilities or his death. He was my comrade, and I loved him! I loved him!"

"Of course you did!" Nolarion pressed the young man back into his chair, and enfolded his son's head against his own great chest. "Of course you did," he repeated soothingly. Endemion rocked against his father's body, his arms wrapped around the older man's waist. I glanced away, not wanting to intrude upon the athlete's grief; the other men did the same. After a few moments Endemion's sobs quieted, and he lifted his head from his father's chiton. Nolarion stared into his son's face closely, then nodded and released him. The magistrate resumed his kline and swallowed several gulps of wine. Endemion sat quietly, reddened eyes downcast.

"In any case," Euphemius said, his head bobbing up and down in time to his words, "numerous persons handled the wine, the jugs, the amphora, and the cups! As absurd as it sounds, the poison could have been placed in a cup by a pouring girl, by one of Crystheus' temporary helpers, or even by one of the spectators, pushing for a closer look at the ceremony. It could even have been done by a bystander along the procession route, handing out sweetmeats or tidbits to the athletes as they went by."

The others nodded at this statement, and I thought to myself that this was a fine kettle of fish, indeed.

"One thing is clear, however," declared Valato. "Many of the people believe that this is a sign that Poseidon is displeased with the festival or, indeed, with all of Ionia. Since the crime is murder, it is the province of the state to solve it, and show the populace that it has nothing to do with the gods' favor or disfavor with the city or Asiatic Greece!" Normally, the solving of a crime is the province of the victim's family, but murder is so serious in its implications that its investigation has been largely preempted by the government. This is not to say that there is a special person or group of persons responsible for the investigation of a crime or for the enforcement of the law — it is just another duty of the city's magistrates.

"I believe something else is equally clear," interjected Euphemius. "Since the act was committed on the grounds of the Panionion, the logical individual to pursue the investigation and bring the culprit to justice is Crystheus!"

At this unexpected pronouncement the major priest jumped to his feet, upsetting his half-full kylix, and protested vociferously, his eyes bulging impressively.

"I cannot do this thing. My duties keep me so occupied that I have no time for anything else. Besides, I know nothing about finding a murderer or investigating a crime, nothing. I have never been near a crime before in my life!"

His hands twisted in the front of his chiton, he glanced wildly about until his gaze rested upon me.

"Wait!" he exclaimed. " I have it. The pollution already resides in Bias, yes, in Bias, since he touched Tyrestes as the young man was dying! His finding the criminal will be both opportune, since he has few important duties, and appropriate, since he may then rid himself of the miasma of death!"

By the gods, those eyes shone as if he had a lamp on the inside of his fat head.

All the other eyes in the andron turned to me, and I could feel their thoughts bounding in upon mine like a hunting dog slavering after a rabbit.

"This is not the right solution," I asserted weakly, looking pleadingly from one to the other. " I hold no special place of respect in the people's minds and have been no nearer crime than Crystheus! Besides, I have plenty to do in keeping the sacred grounds presentable."

The magistrates again glanced at each other, I noticed even Endemion watching me expectantly.

"This may indeed be a viable solution," murmured Nolarion softly. "It is true that the pollution must be rooted out, and that a polluted person has a great stake in doing so."

"In that case, why can't Endemion be your investigator?" I suggested indignantly. "He is as polluted as I am!" Nolarion dismissed this idea with a impatient wave of his beefy hand.

"My son is the only chance left for Priene to win in the games. His miasma will be dispersed, when he takes the pentathlon and brings glory back to the city, as I did many years ago!" The two other magistrates nodded sagely at this bit of nonsense, effectively leaving me high and dry. Crystheus nailed down the lid of my coffin.

"I will use two of the temporary helpers until Bias returns triumphant," he suggested happily. "I have the greatest confidence in his ability to reach a satisfactory, indeed a completely satisfactory, conclusion in this incident." Thank you very much, I thought sourly, glaring at him.

"So then, good Bias," said the bald Valato, putting the matter squarely in my unwelcoming hands, "will you undertake to deliver our city and sacred grounds of this disgrace?"

My gaze sought out each person in the andron in turn, and the answer in each one's eyes was the same.

"Indeed, sir," I sighed in defeat. "I will do my best to solve this problem, and report my findings back to Crystheus, if this pleases you."

They all nodded solemnly, if not with evident relief. This answer to the dilemma had several obvious advantages, even to my untrained and naive mind. If I succeeded, then I would be free of the miasma, and the city and the sacred grounds would be shown to be blameless, since Poseidon would not be hiding the identity of the murderer. If I failed, the magistrates could claim that Poseidon was angry with me alone, or at the most with Crystheus as well, since the murder occurred on the Panionion grounds. At any rate, I and not the city, would retain the pollution, since Poseidon would have chosen not to clear my spirit of this contamination! The festival and games would recover over the next four years, and all Priene need do to exorcise itself was appoint a new major and minor priest. What a monumental balls-up, I thought to myself.

The magistrates were saved from any further inane protestations from me by the startling sound of much wailing and lamenting outside the prodomus of Nolarion's large house. Tyrestes' relatives had arrived to claim his body.

CHAPTER V

How was I to go about this, I wondered? I had no special talents that would help me find this murderer. Come to think of it, I had no special talents at all. Granted, I was a fair athlete, but certainly I was not in the same class as Endemion or the other competitors in the games. I had been learning the business of agriculture since my teen years, and although I was confident I would be a better farmer than my father (which is not saying much), our estate was not large enough to enable me to improve the family's fortunes significantly in that way. I was an absolute loss at the finer arts that a Greek gentleman was supposed to master, those of writing poetry, composing and playing music, and singing. My father had hired several minor sophists over the years to try and teach me the rudiments of these skills, but I had proved a poor pupil, being more interested in the birds and insects outside the classroom window. I was a pretty good hand at hunting, had no problem with reading, and could do enough arithmetic to keep a farm's books. What any of that had to do with solving a crime I could not say, but I supposed one could apply the basics of logic to the problem and watch what might come bobbing to the surface.

I fingered the small piece of vellum I had requested of the magistrates before I trudged home, dejected, from Nolarion's estate that evening. It was, in effect, a warrant, and authorized me to question everyone concerned with the incident. All three magistrates had signed the document, although with some hesitation, perhaps fearing I would make a nuisance of myself with the various dignitaries and athletes attending the festival. It had occurred to me more than once that in the eyes of Priene's government officials, it might be just as well if I did not find Tyrestes' killer. In that case, the blame could easily be shifted to myself and Crystheus and our ineptitude as priests of the Panionion. I rubbed my tired eyes and sighed. Surely, that could not happen—I was just depressed by the whole affair.

I was in our own andron, eating a late dorpon of cheese, olives, and bread laid out for me by Selcra. My sisters had all retired for the night, and I could hear my mother singing softly back in her own bedroom. I stopped worrying for a moment and listened to her lilting voice; she was singing a song of weaving and spinning. My father looked at me from the other kline across the room, shifting his position so that he rested on one elbow.

"Well, my son, how do you intend to go about this?" He was echoing my thoughts exactly. I grinned at him ruefully.

"I am not at all sure, Father. I thought the best place to start would be to speak separately to any of the procession or the crowd that were close to the wine table by the altar gate. One of them could have seen something amiss or out of place." I shrugged, not sure how to continue.

"You don't have much time, you know. The athletic competitions begin tomorrow morning, with the artistic contests spread between the events. To start, you'll have to search out those who were at that location at that time."

"We know that the magistrates, athletes, and wine pouring girls were all there," I countered. "That is where I must begin."

Holicius looked thoughtful for few seconds, and spoke softly. "You must tread very carefully here, boy. Since you were one of the last to touch Tyrestes alive, you know that many people will believe you are polluted by the murder. You will already stand out in the crowd, since you cannot avoid wearing black and cutting your hair short. These things will cause a number of our fellow citizens to regard you warily at best. Add to that the fact that you will be speaking to high-ranking citizens or their relatives, who may be quick to take offense, and you have a volatile situation, to say the least. You must be very cautious in how you approach this issue."

I stared at him, surprised and a little exasperated.

"Father, how will I find any answers if I must be politically careful whenever I speak?"

"It is not whether you will obtain answers, but rather whether you will even be allowed to ask questions in many cases! Even with your so-called warrant, the citizens of this and the other League cities are under no obligation to cooperate with you." He paused, and added quietly, "All I am saying is that you need to conduct your inquiries in such a manner that the possible witnesses or suspects will either want to cooperate or will feel obligated to, at the very least."

"In other words," I reflected wryly," I can catch more flies with honey than with vinegar?"

"Exactly, my son!" His mouth twitched at the corners, but he soberly pointed out, "We do not have many murders in Ionia, thank the gods, but remember, once a murderer has been imbued with the miasma caused by his first killing, it becomes easier for him to strike again."

He rose stiffly, his knee joints popping, adjusted his cloak in the slight evening chill, and chirped cheerfully, "Enough of this for now. I am going to commune with your mother, and then retire. Good night, my son." An embrace, a kiss on the cheek, and he tottered down the hallway toward the sound of Tesessa's soft crooning.

But not enough of it for me, I thought. Mentally, I started a list of those to whom I would need to speak. Unfortunately, right at the top of the list were the three magistrates, Valato, Euphemius, and Nolarion! They were the ones who had held out the cups to the pouring girls, to be filled with red wine and handed to the athletes. I could not imagine what motive one of them might have for committing such a crime, but perhaps one had seen something out of place and a gentle jogging of his memory could jar it loose.

There was Endemion, of course. Although it was known that he and Tyrestes appeared to be the friendliest of rivals, it was also known that he was just a hair less qualified than his friend. I had observed them competing many times over the past year, and it always seemed that Tyrestes could sprint just a stride faster, throw the javelin and discus just a pace further, and punch just that little bit harder in boxing. The two were far and away the best two athletes that Priene had to offer at these games, but with Tyrestes no longer in the competition, Endemion's chances of winning many events were improved *just* that much more. Yes, I would have to question the muscular Endemion.

Then, there were the other athletes, each of whom had crowded up to the tables for his kylix of ritual wine. Would they know anything? By Zeus, there must be a hundred of them, I thought miserably. I knew only a few of their names, but even if I possessed a list of the competitors and their home cities, what an impossible task! Perhaps I could engage Endemion as a source of information, even if he was innocent. He would be familiar with many of the athletes, having met them all at practices over the past week, and could point out which ones had been closest to him and Tyrestes. Must handle Endemion very gently, I reflected.

I supposed that I might be able to get some information from the wine pouring girls. Surely, they would not have poisoned anybody, but then again, what if one of them had been spurned by Tyrestes, or worse, secretly used and then spurned? That could be a reason for murder, could it not? I brightened, remembering that Risalla would know which of the girls had poured at the time that the Priene athletes were crowding up to the table. I would speak to her first thing in the morning.

With this in mind, I tried to think about who else might have seen anything untoward. I was interrupted by the clattering entrance of Duryattes, our young male slave and the son of Selcra and her husband Dryses.

"Pardon, young master." He held out a oinochoai of clear wine mixed with cool water. "Your father sent me in to refresh your kylix."

I watched Duryattes as he poured me more wine. He had been born here on the estate about thirteen years ago. His father Dryses had been a loyal retainer of my father's for over forty years; Holicius had rewarded him by buying Selcra as a wife some fourteen years earlier. Both his parents were Carian by birth, but Duryattes had little of the barbarian about him, having grown up on a Greek estate.

His wits were as sharp as his movements, and the only bad thing I could say about him was that perhaps they were a little too sharp at times. I sometimes had an uneasy feeling that he was laughing at me behind the sleeve of his tunic, so to speak.

"Wait a moment, Duryattes," I commanded as he began to withdraw. "I wish to speak to you."

"Yes, young master?" He looked at me in an amused, but just respectful enough manner, standing straight and tall as a young sapling.

"You know that I am to investigate the murder of the athlete Tyrestes?"

"Oh, yes, young master! I overhead you and the master discussing it over your dorpon a while ago."

"You are familiar with many of the slaves of the city and the gossip that occurs among families of the citizens?"

"Yes, indeed." He stared at me closely for a moment. "Why is the young master asking?"

"The young master is asking because he wants you to join him in apprehending the perpetrator of this foul deed. You know as well as I that the pollution caused by this crime must be dissipated in order to please Poseidon. You can talk with the slaves who were near the altar at the time of the poisoning, while I cannot."

He eyed me cautiously. "But I am sure that the young master could succeed as well as I at that. Besides, you know I have many duties to perform here at your father's estate."

I could see the light from the oil lamps gleaming in his eyes. Oh, yes, he wanted to be in on this, despite his denials.

"Nonsense," I asserted firmly. "You know that the other slaves will tell you much more than they would tell me. Besides, I am certain my father would release your services to me during the games." I paused for the slightest moment, and pretended to hesitate. "Perhaps you're afraid of being infected by the miasma yourself? I couldn't blame you if you're too frightened to assist me."

Duryattes drew himself up indignantly, and answered with all the bravado a thirteen-year-old could muster. "I am not afraid, young master! I'll find these answers for you if they are there to be found. We Carians fear only the gods of our fathers!"

I chopped his words off swiftly at this rejoinder, as it certainly is not wise to tempt the gods too much, be they Carian or in this case, Greek.

"Very well, then," I said calmly. "We shall set out at dawn tomorrow to investigate this evil deed! Your courage is noteworthy. You may withdraw."

"Yes, young master." He turned to go. "I will not fail you." I listened to him hurrying up the hallway back toward the kitchen, and with a gusty sigh, took a swallow of wine. If only my inquiries would be so easy, please the gods!

CHAPTER VI

"THIS IS RIDICULOUS!" I thought sourly the next morning, as I strode in the glaring sunshine through the main gate of the city on my way to the stadium. I fingered the black linen of my tunic with ill-concealed disgust, and ran a hand through my hair. My mother had certainly done a thorough job, I reflected ruefully; I doubted that my hair was more than an inch long anywhere. Mind you, I am not a vain man, but my very average looks were not enhanced by hair as short as a slave's on the sales block. When you consider that Tyrestes had not even been a friend of mine, you might conclude I did not enjoy my parents' insistence that I abide by all the proper observances of grief for the death of a loved one. It would take me a cursed year to grow my hair back so that I could look halfway decent on the streets!

And to make matters worse, it was going to be burning hot on this first day of the games. Even at this early hour of the morning, I could feel the sweat gathering under my arms and on the back of my neck. By midday I would undoubtedly look like a fugitive from one of the acting troupes here for the comedy presentations, with the hastily applied dark dye of my tunic running down my arms and legs. My mood blackened to match the color of my tunic.

Upon arising that morning with an aching head from a combination of too much wine and too much thinking, I had eaten a light ariston breakfast in the rear courtyard just after sunrise. My mother and sisters were already gathered there by the time I grumpily arrived, chattering gaily like so many pretty birds, dressed in their best finery in anticipation of watching several athletic contests and perhaps a few plays today in the city. Tesessa looked at me knowingly, as I flopped down onto a bench and accepted the proffered clay plate from Selcra. My mother looked lovely, her graying hair piled in great profusion on the top of her head and secured in place with long gold pins. Her face was tanned and healthy; she had not yet applied the lead powder she used to whiten her complexion.

"And what will you be up to, my son, as we are observing the festivities?" she inquired. No fool, my mother, she was well aware of what my father and I had been discussing last night. In fact, she probably remembered more about it than I did, considering the lateness of the hour when Holicius had left her bedroom to retire to his own. I smiled at her in a great show of white teeth.

"Why, nothing particular, Mother. I thought I would take Duryattes and go watch the opening foot races in the stadium. Some people might be there I'd like to have a word with."

"Well, you can't go until I cut your hair to a respectful length for a mourner. Selcra dyed a tunic for you last night. You can change into it after ariston." She eyed my snowy white tunic with disapproval.

"You might also take care when you speak to others about this dreadful crime," she added softly, her brow furrowing with concern. She touched me lightly on the arm as I stuffed a fig into my mouth. I smiled at her and nodded. She turned to call to my sister Risalla.

"Risalla, come here, child, and speak to your brother." She motioned with a shapely hand for her third daughter to sit beside me on the bench. Risalla threw herself on the seat with a jarring thump, and her rosy face beamed happily up at me. I peered at her dubiously, smearing some honey on a thick piece of bread. Risalla's good nature was almost annoying at times. One came away from her with the feeling that one could get knocked over backwards if one was not careful. It was not that I disliked her; it was rather that the combination of her wide smile and vacant eyes tended to whittle my temper to a fine edge.

"Let us talk about yesterday at the altar ceremony," I suggested quietly. Her ebullient manner dampened as she looked away from me and stared at the ground. As a country girl she was familiar with suffering and death, but there is unquestionably a great difference between the end of life for an animal and the death of a man.

"I don't know what I can tell you," she whispered. " I only saw Tyrestes fall down and then you gathered him into your arms. I didn't see anything else."

"I'm not so much concerned by what you saw when he died," I said, "as I am with what you may have observed or heard prior to his actual death." She quickly raised her eyes from the ground, and stared at me.

"What do you mean?" she asked, her lower lip trembling. I laid my plate aside, and took her hand in mine.

"I want to know what you may have seen or heard during the procession or at the wine pouring ceremony that might help me in my investigation. You know that I have been charged with finding the foul individual who committed this terrible crime?" She nodded slightly, her eyes beginning to shine with unshed tears.

"Think back to the wine pouring yesterday," I suggested. "Did you see, perhaps, anybody handle a cup strangely or place anything in a cup before or after one of you girls poured wine for the athletes?"

She thought for a moment, then shook her head vigorously, her curls bouncing on her shoulders. With her mind on a subject other than Tyrestes' death, she brightened a bit.

"No, I can't remember anything like that, but it was so exciting and crowded, that I suppose someone could have mishandled a cup and I wouldn't have noticed. I was very busy pouring myself, you know, and I poured for more athletes than any other girl!" A wide smile broke out on her sun-dappled face as she recalled the glorious moment. I bit my tongue, not wanting to frighten her by my impatience.

"Quite so," I told her, "and it was well-deserved too. Do you remember who gave the cup of wine to Tyrestes himself?"

Risalla thought about it for several long moments. Then she shook her head again.

"It was one of the magistrates, of course, but I don't know which one. I'm sorry, Bias, but everything was so exciting, and there were other people gathered around besides the athletes. I was so busy pouring that I just did not notice."

"What about the procession itself? Did you talk to any of the other girls during or before the parade?"

My sister laughed at this, and flounced her curls with both hands, recalling the colorful clothes, exotic perfumes, and many handsome men and beautiful girls.

"Oh, yes! It was wonderful and fascinating! There were so many of my friends and so many lovely men there! I must have spoken to a hundred of them!" She clapped her hands at the memory. I smiled weakly and looked at my mother for assistance.

"Daughter," she said firmly. "Did you speak to any of the girls about any liaisons they may have had with any of the athletes?"

"Liaisons?" echoed Risalla, glancing at Tesessa. "What do you mean, liaisons?"

My mother sighed. "I mean, did any of the girls confide in you about love affairs with the young men? I was once your age, Daughter. I do know what young women talk about to each other in the rare moments they are together and away from their men!"

Risalla blushed furiously, and wound her hands in the folds of her chiton. She did not meet my mother's eyes.

"Oh, no, Mother," she protested feebly. "I have never talked to anyone about such things!" My mother, knowing that this was exactly what my precocious, robust sister *would* talk about, grimaced and then grasped Risalla's chin with her hand, forcing her to look into her eyes.

"Don't play with me, Daughter. Your brother is charged with a serious responsibility; the outcome could affect the honor and reputation of this family! Let me ask again — who did you speak to about their doings with the athletes?"

At this, Risalla burst into tears, and threw herself into my mother's arms. Tesessa patted her on the back and murmured soothingly to her until the sobs resolved themselves into gulps and sniffs. At last, my sister freed herself from my mother's embrace, still clutching Tesessa's hands.

"There were only a few who knew anything about men," Risalla said. "But they all pretended they did. I don't know who was serious and who was joking."

"Which of the girls do you think may have actually met with an athlete and gone beyond mere conversation?" I asked baldly. "Think, Risalla!"

My sister's distress was now turning to curiosity. I had a fleeting thought that perhaps she was not quite so empty-headed as I believed. She reflected on the problem for several minutes, smoothing the folds of her chiton about her sturdy body.

"Well, there were several girls who bragged about their introductions. But none of them actually said they had done anything."

I sighed with pent-up exasperation, and started to rise. My sister forestalled me by lifting her hand slightly in my direction.

"There were two girls who appeared to know more than the rest of us," she said, looking at my mother, who nodded encouragingly at her.

"How do you mean, 'know more'?" I asked impatiently. My mother shot a quick glance at me that clearly said — be silent and wait.

"Two of the wine girls gave the rest of us the impression that they really knew what they were talking about. I mean, all of us know about how things are done. . . . But these girls seemed to . . . seemed to . . ." She did not finish the sentence.

Tesessa looked at me with a slight but clearly triumphant smile.

"Who are these girls?" I inquired gently, clasping one of Risalla's hands, holding it closely with both of mine. My mother nodded at me approvingly over my sister's shoulder.

"One is Bilassa, Kreton's daughter, and the other is Valato's daughter, Ossadia," she said finally. I heard Tesessa's sharp intake of breath.

"Now listen carefully," I said, looking into Risalla's eyes. "Did either of them mention any athletes' names?"

She considered me deeply for a moment, and then the light of understanding dawned in her eyes. I swear I could see it, like the sun bursting over the top of a hill to dispel the night. She gripped my hands tightly.

"Not by name. That would never do! But perhaps in another way! One of them said she was involved with an athlete from Miletus, but the other one hinted that her admirer was one of the competitors from Priene!"

But she could not tell me which girl was dallying with the Miletian athlete and which with the homegrown boy. Even my mother's gentle prodding failed to penetrate my sister's whirling memories of those few moments in such an exciting day. And so, as I entered the western gate to the city of Priene, I had two more to add to those I should question. And to make matters more difficult, they were the daughters of two prominent citizens of the state!

It would be a miracle if the fathers permitted me to speak to their daughters on any subject, let alone on the subject of possible murder. Would any father believe that his daughter had dallied with a young man prior to marriage, much less murdered the young man later on? I almost laughed aloud when I considered the prospects of my broaching the subject to the two fathers. Valato, of course, I have already mentioned. He was one of the city magistrates, he of the bald head, short light brown beard, and cutting and sarcastic remarks. I shuddered to think what would happen if I approached him and informed him humbly that his daughter had been fooling around with a young man, perhaps even the murdered Tyrestes. Gods, the investigation would be over in a heartbeat and my future in Priene would go with it!

The other father was, if anything, even worse than Valato. Kreton was an aristocratic landowner whose estates were among the richest in the Maeander Valley. His horses were known far and wide, rivalling the best that Colophon had to offer, and his grape vineyards produced some of the finest wines this side of Chios. Physically, he was a huge man, capable of breaking normal mortals such as me like a stick with his bare hands, and in addition, he had three huge sons who were equally ferocious. In fact, Krelonan, the eldest of the three, was the champion wrestler of Priene, widely expected to win the heavy class championship at the games. I could just see myself asking to speak to the beautiful Bilassa, and being hounded through the olive groves by these three baying giants.

Considering these various scenarios, I eliminated the possibility of directly approaching the two lovelies, and decided instead to seek out the magistrates for private conversations. Although the waters in that direction were potentially also dangerous, perhaps I could smooth them with logical thoughts and patriotic gestures.

The probable location of Valato, Nolarion, and Euphemius was not hard to determine. This being the opening day of the games, they would be at the stadium to observe the initial footrace and jumping competitions. With Tyrestes doing all *his* athletics against other shades in Hades, Priene's greatest hope in the combined events lay in the prowess of Endemion, and all the citizens of the city would be there to cheer him on, as well as support the other athletes in the individual events.

Simultaneously, I had unleashed Duryattes with instructions to seek out any slaves who had been present at the wine pouring ceremony. He had accompanied me as far as the city gate, and then had made tracks for the agora, the market place, where we knew he would find other servants eager to fill in each other's gaps of knowledge and rumor about the murder of Tyrestes. Duryattes' quick and cunning mind would function best in the shadow slave world of innuendo and rumor that seethed below the daylight world of the citizen. But before we had left the house that morning my father had pointed out that I was not free to subject the boy to dangers without his permission. Yawning and rubbing his eyes, he had wandered out into the courtyard for his ariston, just as I was preparing to leave with Duryattes.

"Take great care with how you use the lad," cautioned Holicius, wagging a warning finger in my face as he nibbled on a chunk of goat cheese and popped an olive into his mouth. "I have known his father Dryses since I was a youngster. As you know, we grew up together, and he was my constant companion and guardian. It would grieve him greatly, if his only child were to come to some harm because of you."

I regarded my father gravely, as I considered the import of his statement. He was a firm believer in the superiority of the Greek over the barbarian, even barbarians as Hellenized as the Lydians. On the other hand, he also believed that we had a solemn responsibility to those who belonged to our family, and this responsibility included insuring they were as happy and healthy as possible in the context of their situation. He was particularly fond of Duryattes, whom he saw as the living embodiment of his gift of Selcra to his lifelong companion, Dryses.

"I promise not to put him in any danger, Father," I pledged. "I plan to have him talk only with the other slaves to try to dig beneath the surface of this crime. You know it is likely that slaves and servants have information that is not available to me, but could be yielded up to him. I will make sure that he is not involved in any physical danger."

"And yourself, as well!" added Holicius, tugging at his beard. "Do you remember what I said last night? Dark thoughts will burrow underground in the light of day, but they will still be there, watching and waiting."

CHAPTER VII

"BY HADES, THIS CERTAINLY is not the right way to start the games," boomed Valato, staring angrily down the length of the stadium. His small frame quivered with indignation as one of Priene's entries in the initial stadium sprints came in dead last in the first of the qualifying races. The hapless Priene athlete could be seen standing at the end of the large, oval structure, his head hanging down and his hands on his hips. By not finishing in the top one-half of his first heat, he had already been eliminated from the next set of heats designed to narrow the field continuously until the single-stadium-length championship race. Of course, there were still the diaulos or double-length sprints and the long race to come, but Valato obviously did not believe that this particular contestant would bring much glory to the home city.

"When does the next sprint begin?" he growled to me, taking a gulp of wine from the kylix he gripped in his small fist. He vigorously rubbed the top of his bald head in frustration.

"It appears that they are lining up now, Magistrate," I replied, pointing at the starting line. The next set of sprinters were already gathering at the line at the other end of the stadium, stretching and flexing their nude bodies in the morning sun. The stadium was even now almost filled with cheering, chattering, shouting spectators from all over Ionia, and this was just the beginning race of the beginning day. I thought ruefully that the death of Tyrestes had not noticeably dampened the enthusiasm of the visitors and local citizens for sport.

"Are any of our young men in this heat?" Valato asked, squinting at the athletes. It struck me that his vision might not be as strong as it had been, and he could not make out the features of the contestants. They were about a half-stade, say 120 paces, from us at the far end of the stadium.

"No, sir," I assured him. "Our next entry is Endemion, who is in the fourth heat."

He plopped back down on the seat, taking another swallow of his watered wine. The wine sellers, their oinochoai jugs brimming with refreshing wine straight from stout psykters buried in the ground, were already doing a roaring trade. I spied several of them moving about the stands loudly plying their wares, and motioned one of them over to me.

"Some more wine, sir?" I asked Valato in my most obsequious tone, as the seller approached.

"Yes, thank you, young Bias." He held out his kylix. The seller refilled his cup, and then gave me one as well. I passed a few stater into his outstretched hand.

I had found Valato almost as soon as I had entered the stadium, entering it from the river side. The structure crouched on the flat ground next to the Maeander on the east side of the city, its long axis paralleling the riverfront. Valato and his family sat in desirable seats almost at the center of the stands, close to the ground.

His wife, Myrnia, a slight, stout woman with hair the color of newly-turned soil ready for planting had smiled to welcome me, as I descended the steps between the rows of seats and greeted the magistrate. Valato had grunted at me, intent on watching the first heat of the day, and motioned me impatiently to a seat. I paid my respects to Myrnia, and then turned to Valato's children.

His eldest daughter Ossadia, she who Risalla said "knew" about "adventures" with men, stared indifferently at me for a moment, before she turned her attention back to the race. She was about fifteen years old, possessed her father's light brown hair and her mother's tendency to put on weight. Oh, she was attractive enough in a kind of bored, washed-out way, but hardly beautiful. She did have an attractive if solid figure, and her complexion was clear and unblemished even though she wore no whitening makeup. Her bright blue eyes were an asset, I suppose. Her hands, by contrast with the rest of her body, were long and slender, the fingers coiled like small white snakes in her lap.

Seated next to her on the hard stand was her younger brother by four years, Illanos, and her small sister, Xenia. They were already bouncing up and down on their cushions in anticipation of the first race. Normally, women and children would not be seen in public like this, but these *were* the great Panionic games and many general restrictions fell by the wayside in the excitement of the celebrations.

"I don't think these next few heats will be of much interest," I remarked offhandedly, taking a sip of wine. "Might I speak to you for a moment, Valato?"

The small man grunted his assent, and rose to walk down to the stadium turf, where only the rich and powerful were allowed to mingle with the waiting athletes. I followed him down, receiving another distant smile from his wife and another indifferent glance from his daughter.

"What is it you wish, Bias?" he asked, letting his eyes rove up and down the field, gauging the various athletes assembled in small knots about the grounds.

"Sir, as you know, I have begun pursuing the murder of the unfortunate Tyrestes, and in the spirit of gaining background information, wondered if I might ask you what you might know about his character and personality." I mentally crossed my fingers, hoping this was the right approach to use with the diminutive official. Apparently, I guessed correctly, because he replied without hesitation, shading his eyes with his hand as he peered at the far end of the stadium. "Well, I did not know him as well as I knew the father. I'm not sure that I can tell you anything to help you."

"Sir, since at present I am utterly in the dark in this matter, anything you can add to dispel the shadows will be of assistance."

"Very well, then. As I say, I didn't know him well. Oh, I have watched him grow up over the years, as I and his father, Tirachos, worked together as soldiers and fellow aristocrats, and he seemed like a good boy on the whole. Perhaps a little headstrong, but many boys are like that until they reach manhood, eh? I know that he took his father's death like a true man several years ago and made sure that all the proprieties were observed in his family. He was the eldest son, and the family has a small estate out toward the coast from the city. I suppose the second son, Usthius, will inherit the land now, since Tyrestes was not married."

"I suppose your family must have associated socially with his family over the years," I said.

"Oh, yes. As I have said, Tirachos and I knew each other for years, in a companionable, if not close way. His family visited us several times, and we returned the visits a few times, as I recall."

"Do you recall the last time this occurred?" I assumed my best offhand manner, glancing down the other length of the stadium to where the race officials were waiting impatiently for the next heat to begin. He frowned in thought for a moment.

"It must have been about six months ago. Perhaps in the fall during the month of Pyanopsion. Yes, I believe it was at the last Apaturian festival. Of course, Tirachos was long dead by then. As I remember, Tyrestes' younger brother Usthius was being accepted into the phratry at that time. We are in the same phratry, you know." The phratries are the modern versions of the old mainland Greek tribes, and draw powerful loyalty from the old aristocratic families.

I paused, as we watched the straining runners of the second race flash by. An athlete from Erythrae barely beat out a rival from Samos.

"So your family members knew each other as well?" I asked casually, staring down toward the finish line, where the judges were arguing vociferously about the outcome of the race. The Erythraen and Samosian athletes hovered expectantly at the edge of the judges' discussion.

"They knew each other slightly as children," Valato answered vaguely, his attention now turned back to the starting area, where the third heat contestants were readying themselves. "Why do you ask?"

"Oh, no special reason." I brushed his question away with a wave of my hand. "I just thought I might be able to obtain some useful information about Tyrestes from your family, with your permission. You know that sometimes young people will tell each other things that they will not mention to older folks. Perhaps I could learn something about Tyrestes from Ossadia, if they spoke together at all."

Valato turned his full attention to me for the first time, his mild eyes sharpening.

"You wish to speak to my daughter about Tyrestes? Why do you think she might be able to help you?"

I could feel the sweat forming on my forehead. I made a point of shading my eyes and peering down the length of the stadium to the starting line.

"Oh, I just thought he might have spoken to her about his acquaintances or ambitions," I tried to speak calmly. "Ossadia is a pretty girl, and men tend to brag to pretty girls, eh?" I chuckled nervously. Valato continued to contemplate me with interest.

"I suppose he could have told her about himself," he said thoughtfully. "I did let them speak alone in our back courtyard several times, in the hope that he would approach me as the head of his family with a view to uniting himself or his brother, Usthius, with our family by marrying Ossadia. All quite proper, of course. But he never said anything about that. It would have been a desirable match. My family is quite old and respected, you know."

"Of course, sir. I can see that the match would have been a lucky one for Tyrestes' family. But your family could probably find a more suitable alliance. Any father in Priene would be proud to link the family of Valato with his own." I smiled obsequiously.

Valato turned his attention back to the athletes, who were just getting into starting positions for the third race.

"You are quite right that any family would benefit by being linked to my family," he said. "Yes, I suppose you might ask Ossadia a few questions, if you believe it will help your inquiries. I must admit I myself thought well of Tyrestes, all in all, but nothing came of my 'fishing'." He turned his attention back to me for a moment, and regarded me with speculative interest.

"You are the eldest son in your family, aren't you, Bias?" he asked innocently.

⁂

The third race had produced no surprises. The favorite runner, a leggy boy from Colophon, won easily, making the other athletes look as if they were on a leisurely stroll.

I stood next to Ossadia at the river entrance to the stadium, and handed her a kylix of weak wine and water. She accepted the cup without much interest. A hulking male slave escort stood just out of earshot, with his attention focused on the athletic action below. Several tendrils of Ossadia's wispy hair danced lightly in the faint breeze wafting through the entrance tunnel.

"Father says I am to cooperate with you if I know anything about Tyrestes that may aid you in your murder inquiry. I'm sure I cannot imagine what it is you think I might know about him."

"I don't expect any information in particular." I paused to sip nonchalantly from my kylix. "But your father did say that he had permitted Tyrestes to speak with you alone a time or two. I was just wondering if he mentioned anything to you about his intentions in the games or, indeed, about his life in general?" She frowned slightly at this, but did not answer me. I hurried on.

"What I mean is that I know a man boasts about his prowess and accomplishments to a pretty girl. Being a man myself, I can see why he might have spoken of such things easily to an attractive and propertied woman such as yourself." I swallowed and beamed at her, hoping I was not being too obvious.

She looked at me closely for a moment, apparently decided I was sincere, smiled slighty, and patted her hair.

"Well, he was quite interested in me and my dowry when I last saw him. That would have been, um, during the last Apaturian festival, about six months ago." She took a very deep breath, watching as my eyes automatically focused on her rising bosom under her thin chiton. I flicked my eyes away, but not before she allowed herself another smile.

"And did he speak at all of his desires for the future?" Wrong word, idiot, I thought, as I saw her gaze sharpen.

"What sort of *desires*, Bias?" she whispered with a sort of hiss at the end of my name. With a slender finger she slowly wiped a slight sheen of perspiration from the down above her upper lip.

"Not *desires* perhaps," I stumbled on, "but plans or intentions. I mean, can you recall if he spoke of what he planned to do at the games or in the near future?"

"We spoke of many things." I nervously noted just the beginning of a spark seeming to ignite in her eyes, as she took the tiniest step toward me. By the gods, I speculated to myself, what is hidden beneath that plain face?

"He was very ambitious, you know," she continued. "He planned to be the winner of the Panionic Games, and use that fame to secure a wife from a desirable family. His estate was not the largest one in the area." She sniffed derisively.

"Were you one of his candidates?" I watched with fascination the flame smoulder in those now very attractive eyes. "Your father is both rich and famous, and I am sure he will provide you with an excellent dowry." Her tongue flicked out to lick her lips. By Poseidon, it was like observing the performance of a consummate actor playing a harlot, but I was under no illusions that Ossadia was acting. I could almost *smell* the scent of suppressed passion. It was pleasantly cool in that entranceway, but I was beginning to sweat again.

"Yes, he was interested in me for my position and the advantages that might offer him." Her gaze never left my face for a heartbeat. I began to feel like a squirrel hypnotized by a snake. "I know my father saw no great obstacles to such a union."

"And yourself?" I wheezed, edging backwards toward the tunnel wall. It did not do me any good. For every miniscule step I retreated, she slid forward the same distance, her wonderful bosom rising and falling with increasing rapidity.

"It didn't make any difference what I thought," she asserted, her tongue flicking out again. "It only made a difference what my father thought. But if you must know, I did not particularly care for him. He boasted too much. He went on and on about athletic competitions and his need for more land. His land adjoins Kreton's, you know, and I'm sure he would have welcomed an alliance with that boor."

Where had I ever got the idea that this woman was plain, I thought fleetingly? Her eyes were opened very wide now and blazing intensely blue, and I found I could not look away.

"Of course, he was physically attractive," she acknowledged, as if daring me to pursue that statement. "One certainly could have done worse for a husband than Priene's best athlete."

"Forgive me for asking," I croaked, backed up against the wall of the tunnel, "but did he ever attempt to use that physical beauty to, um, persuade you of his desires?" I used that word again!

An amused smile played over her mouth, as she sidled one step closer. She was now almost against me, looking up into my face. The fingertips of her right hand rested oh so lightly on her breast. The tunnel seemed to have narrowed down, compressing the air so that it became more and more difficult to breathe.

"Persuade me of his desires? If you mean, did he attempt to make love to me, the answer is . . . yes. If you mean, did he make love to me, the answer is . . . no. I have lain with no man. Yet. As I said, I did not particularly care for him. Are you shocked at my honesty? Why did you want to know, Bias?" The slight breeze blew a wisp of her hair against my cheek, like the touch of a spider web.

"I was merely trying to obtain a picture of his character and personality," I stammered, determined to regain the initiative. "He could have used the same approach on any girl that he used with you." My breath caught in my throat, as Ossadia leaned toward me.

"And if he succeeded in making love to her as part of it," she interrupted, staring unblinking up at me, "that might be motive for murder? I think you men overestimate the importance of the first act of lovemaking to a woman."

"Perhaps so," I agreed quickly, "but do I overestimate the effect it might have on the girl's father and family?" She considered this for a moment, and nodded slightly in agreement.

"Yes, I see your point there. And yet, since it did not happen to me, you must seek your insulted family elsewhere."

Ossadia reached out and her long, slender fingers fluttered against my chest for just a moment, burning through the front of my tunic, and then those smoldering eyes glanced down to see that the color of my raiment was the black of mourning. The hand was snatched back as if scalded by the dark cloth. Curtains fell instantly over the fiery eyes, and she was amazingly once again the plain, bored daughter of a rich magistrate. To clear my head, I mentally shook myself like a dog coming out of the water. She stepped back, indifference washed back over her like a wave, and she turned to walk back to the family seats in the stadium. I stood quite still, staring after her, and she paused for a moment, to address me over her shoulder.

"I would like very much to see this next race. Habiliates of Miletus will be running. If you want my opinion of physical attractiveness in a man, look at him and you will find it. He is easily Tyrestes' match." She turned and looked at me. "If he were to try and, shall we say, persuade me of his desires, I believe I could be persuaded, propriety or not."

CHAPTER VIII

My conversations with Valato and his mercurial daughter left me with an understandable thirst and a healthy appetite as well. I hurriedly downed several kylixes of wine from one of the local wine-sellers, as I pondered Ossadia's pointed statement about the abilities of Habiliates of Miletus. He easily won his initial running heat, of course, and I watched her in the stadium stands, yelling lustily with the best of them, as he sprinted across the finish line paces ahead of the second-place man. She hugged herself with strong arms, as he strutted past the stadium seats, and I could imagine those eyes burning brightly as they devoured him from a distance. Had she done more than just admire those rippling muscles from afar? If she was one of Risalla's adventuresses, then it would appear that she would be the one who was interested in "a Miletian athlete." That would leave Bilassa, the beautiful daughter and sister of the house of Kreton, as the knowing partner of a local boy, hopefully named Tyrestes. But it was all so questionable. My impression was that once Ossadia's fires got stoked, a mere mortal man would not be able to tell if she was telling the truth or not.

I satisfied a gnawing hunger with some maza bread made from barley grain paste mixed with olives, cheese, and eggs, and then searched the stands for the other magistrates, Euphemius or Nolarion. There were now fully five thousand noisy spectators in the stadium, but the wealthy of Priene would be spreading their prosperous bottoms on the best seats. I spied the father of Endemion on the other side of the stadium after an hour of searching. His son had easily won his heat in the single-length races. The opening contests of wrestling and boxing were slated for this afternoon, and most of the married women had left for a play or musical interlude in the city, this rougher type of sport being considered unseemly for already committed eyes to see. There were still a number of unmarried girls and women in the audience, encouraged by custom to view the "natural state" of men, in order to think about what they should hope for in a husband. I was not surprised to notice that Ossadia remained to observe the afternoon's entertainment, and indeed, had moved down to the end of the stadium where the boxing bouts would be held.

My mother considered it inappropriate for her younger daughters to view bloodletting at an early age and had left with Tirah, Tapho, and Elissa in hand, the eldest bawling piercingly that she should be able to stay, since she was now twelve years old and almost a woman. Risalla was left in the care of my father and a very disdainful Arlana, whom I noticed was watching the flexing wrestlers from the corner of her eyes even as she pretended to look away. Risalla was not even trying to pretend, but was staring hungrily at a particularly large specimen from Chios and folding her arms tightly across her bosom. Holicius wanted to watch the boxing, but after a warning word from Tesessa before she left, had reluctantly moved to the wrestling end of the stadium. I did not see my eldest sister Ulania; I supposed she had left to view a play with our male slave Dryses as escort. I couldn't see her weak-chinned betrothed wanting to stay for either the boxing or the wrestling, and considered he would probably trail after her, properly ignored by both her and Dryses.

Catching sight of Nolarion, I fought my way toward him through the enthusiastic crowd, hoping to be able to speak to him before a Priene athlete competed again. No luck. Endemion was one of the first in the pot for the wrestling competition, and his father naturally had eyes only for him and his match.

There were three wrestling contests going on simultaneously at that end of the stadium, and three boxing competitions proceeding at the opposite end. The wrestling was of the upright variety, with each athlete grappling manfully with his opponent and attempting to throw him to the turf. The judge counted a fall as soon as any part of the body above the knee touched the ground, and watched closely for improprieties like eye or mouth gouging, biting, kicking, strangling, or tripping. Any competitor who attempted any of these illegal acts, was rewarded by the judge with a stinging blow to the back by a flexible wooden rod and a stern warning that another such violation would disqualify him. As you can imagine, this tended to make the wrestling competition fair and above board. Three of five falls were necessary for a victory.

Boxing, on the other hand, was bloody and grueling. There were no rounds in the boxing competition—the athletes just went at it tooth and nail until one surrendered. As with the wrestling, there were three sets of boxers trading blows simultaneously. It was arranged so that different age groups fought at the same time in the different matches. Bands of hard leather were wrapped around the boxers' wrists and over their knuckles in order to reinforce their blows and draw blood. They aimed at the head, rather than the body. I have seen many a boxer fight on until he literally could not see because of the blood flowing into his eyes from the cuts in his forehead.

I reached the big magistrate just as Endemion dispatched his foe for the third time by tossing him over his right shoulder with a mighty heave. The home crowd erupted in rapturous screams, as the victorious athlete danced about the field, his muscular arms raised above his head in victory. Nolarion was shouting madly and stomping his huge feet on the stone flooring.

"My boy, my boy!' he screamed, clenching and unclenching his monstrous fists. "My boy!" His big face was red with exertion, and spittle flew from his lips. Those next to him were pounding him on the back in congratulation, as Endemion strode grinning off the field.

"Sir, sir!" I shouted as the noise began to die, "Congratulations on your son's victory!"

He stared at me as if coming out of a trance, and then beamed a great smile and grabbed me in a bearlike embrace. I felt as if my ribs were beginning to crack when he released me, allowing me to sink on to the seat next to him.

"Well done, sir, well done," I wheezed, as I struggled to catch my breath. Nolarion continued to bask in the praise of many neighbors, who went on congratulating him on his son's magnificent early win. It was as if he himself had won the match, but such is the way of fathers, justly or unjustly accepting some of the credit for their sons' accomplishments.

"He is just like you, Nolarion, just like you twenty years ago," cackled one old white-bearded man, throwing his arms around the magistrate from behind. Nolarion boomed out a great laugh, and twisted about to kiss the ancient on the forehead.

"No, he is better than me, better! He will bring great honor to our city!" The crowd ebbed and flowed about Nolarion, adding their congratulations and praise and then drifting back to their seats to await the next bout. He finally noticed me and motioned for me to sit down beside him.

"What did you think of that, young Bias, eh?" he asked with infectious good humor. I found myself grinning back at him, as he reached up to tousle my close-cropped hair.

"Outstanding, sir, outstanding! You certainly have a son to be proud of in Endemion." He nodded vigorously several times, and then rose to his massive feet in a renewed burst of energy.

"Come on, boy!" he roared, jerking me off the seat I had just occupied. "Let's have a drink to celebrate his victory and go seek him out!" I hurried after him, as he headed for the nearest wine-seller. He thrust a full kylix of wine into my hands, and drained his own in a single swallow. His big hand rubbed energetically at the red wine dribbling into his full-flowing beard.

"Well, by the gods, that was something, eh?" he said. "I think Endemion has a good chance of winning that competition! Let's go find him!"

"Magistrate, please, a moment of your time before we search for him?" I begged. "I would like to ask you a few questions about Tyrestes, if I may?"

Nolarion stopped smiling and stared at me curiously for an instant, and then the huge grin reappeared.

"Of course, young Bias, of course. Come, let us sit over here out of the way, and have some more wine." He indicated an empty pair of seats close by, and motioned for the wine-seller to refill our kylixes. I did not tell him that I probably had had quite enough wine for the moment, and found myself with another overflowing cup. I sipped slowly, rapidly marshalling my thoughts, as I watched him observing me with great good humor.

"Sir," I began, "I am not sure how to proceed with this, but as you yourself pointed out last night, the magistrates were the last people to touch the wine cups before they were given to the athletes at the sacrifice ceremony. You must have had ample opportunity to look about and see who else was in the vicinity of the wine pouring."

Nolarion visibly focused his attention away from his son and on the matter at hand. He wrapped a hamlike fist around his beard and tugged at it thoughtfully..

"Well, yes, that is true, I suppose," he mused. "But I do not recall seeing any angry or disturbed spectators around."

"They wouldn't have to be angry. Was there anybody there who seemed to be out of place?"

"But even if there was, he would have had to have access to the wine cups, would he not? The poison had to be in the cup, since many athletes drank from each oinochoai. The girls there poured wine indiscriminately for all the athletes."

"But did they, sir? Could it have been possible for one of the pourers to give Tyrestes a drink from one jug and then set it aside, even though it was not empty?"

At this point the crowd erupted in a screaming frenzy as Krelonan, the gigantic son of the gigantic Kreton, threw his opponent from Samos to the ground with a bonebreaking thud. The Samosian did not even stir as Krelonan stepped on his chest with a monstrous foot, and threw his arms into the air, basking in the throng's adulation. Nolarion leaped to his feet with the others, and howled his approval of the young Prienian's triumph.

"By the gods, we can't lose in this wrestling competition," he exulted. "With Endemion in the middleweight class and Krelonan in the heavy class, we should take the whole thing!" He thumped back into his seat, and downed several more gulps of wine, before he focused on me again.

"I beg your pardon, Bias," he said with a winning smile. "What was that last question?" I asked him again about the possibility of Tyrestes being the only one to drink from a certain jug. He gazed thoughtfully at the boxing end of the stadium.

"Well, yes, I suppose that is possible. There were many oinochoai jugs there at the pouring. I saw several kicked over in the excitement, and certainly, there was almost as much wine poured onto the ground as into the cups. But wouldn't that mean that the poisoner is one of the wine-pouring girls?"

I paused for a moment, looking into his eyes. His smile was gone.

"Yes, sir, that is exactly what it would mean," I said. "Unless Tyrestes ate some type of deadly food along the road to the Panionion, he had to have ingested the poison in the wine at the altar site. Since the liquid that we drink is turned into blood very quickly, if he had taken a poisoned drink on the road, he never would have reached the religious grounds at all. And it seems to me that to try to give a specific person poisoned food on the road while hundreds of people march by would be very difficult, if it could be done at all. On the other hand, it could be done at the altar site by a very determined person. The killing potion could be placed in a cup to be mixed with the innocent wine as it came from the jug, or it could have been in the jug itself."

Nolarion regarded me very carefully for a moment.

"Then the wine girls are not the only suspects," he remarked at last. "They could have poisoned Tyrestes only if the wine was in a jug, and if that jug was used for his cup alone, and then discarded. The only others who could have had the opportunity to give him poison within a single cup were the magistrates, including myself."

"Yes, sir, " I breathed softly. "Including yourself. Anybody else would either have been noticed or would not have had sufficient access to the jugs or cups." I waited for the proverbial blow to fall. I do not know why I revealed my suspicions to Nolarion and not to Valato earlier. Nolarion's eyes roamed the stadium, and I wondered if he were searching for his fellow magistrates. His answer, when it came, surprised me with its mildness.

"I think you are quite correct," he agreed quietly, still looking off into the distance. "I don't think any other person would have had the time or opportunity to administer the poison and make sure it was given to one chosen victim. Either a wine girl placed it in a jug or one of us magistrates placed it in a cup."

"Sir, perhaps you can help more than you know. Do you happen to recall who gave the cup of wine to Tyrestes at the altar?"

He transferred his gaze from the boxers to my eyes, and then grinned hugely again.

"I remember well who gave the cup to Tyrestes because it was the same magistrate who gave a cup to my son, Endemion, since they stood together in the line. *I* gave the poisoned wine to Tyrestes." He laughed until the tears rolled down his hard face, the guffaws turning to sobs.

CHAPTER IX

ENDEMION'S WRESTLING MATCH was his last event of the day. After eating three hen's eggs, several flat maza bread, and a hefty bowl of yoghurt for the midday deipnon meal, I went searching for him. Another Priene athlete told me Endemion would probably be at the outdoor gymnasium, stretching his muscles with some light running and jumping. I knew that tomorrow he was scheduled to compete in the initial diaulos double-stadium-length foot races in the morning and the chariot racing in the afternoon at the hippodrome, so I sauntered over to the open ground that served as the city's gymnasium.

We Ionians can be a very emotional people, so Nolarion's abrupt transition from laughter to tears did not strike me as odd. After all, comedy and tragedy are separated by the narrowest of margins, wouldn't you say? At any rate, the magistrate had gone on to assure me that he had not been the one to administer the fatal dose to Tyrestes. Nor had he been able to remember which wine girl had poured the libation into the two cups he had held out for Tyrestes and Endemion. Had it been the plain Ossadia or the beautiful Bilassa? Or some other young woman whom I knew nothing about? Even my sister Risalla was there pouring wine!

He could not say. He did admit he shuddered every time he thought about how easy it would have been for the two athletes to have taken the opposite cups he held out—in that case it would have been his son lying cold as a day-old mackerel, instead of competing for the glory of the city of Priene.

I mulled this over, as I strolled through the narrow streets of the eastern edge of the town toward the gymnasium area. Of course, there was no telling if Nolarion was speaking truth. He could easily be lying through his aristocratic teeth. I had to admit that it didn't seem likely that he would falsify his account of actually handing the cups to the two athletes, since I couldn't see that he had much to gain by admitting that he was the one who gave Tyrestes the deadly elixir. It would seem to throw suspicion directly on him. On the other hand, I knew that he was a fiercely loyal friend of both Valato and Euphemius and had been for a number of years. My father told me once, that the only reason Euphemius had been elected to the magistrate's office was that he had been sponsored and praised by his old friend Nolarion. Would that be sufficient reason to lie and say he had poured the dose, when it had actually been done by an old trusted comrade? And, of course, there were the wine girls themselves. Did Nolarion actually know who had poured the nectar into Tyrestes' kylix? Could it have been the daughter of a fellow respected magistrate or that of a fellow aristocrat?

The more I mulled over the possibilities, the more I realized that solving this crime was likely to prove to be a task as daunting as one of the labors of Hercules, though granted his were more muscular than intellectual. Better him than me.

Popping out of a narrow side street, I strode onto the broad field of Priene's gymnasium. It was a large area of flat cleared ground bounded on the west by the outlying houses of the city and on the east by a small creek that flowed from a spring bubbling up from beneath a pile of boulders. The field was used for athletic practice and military drill, and the stream was handy for quenching one's thirst or for bathing at the north corner of the grounds. On the gymnasium's northern edge was a simple shrine to Apollo surrounded by a small sacred grove of olive trees. Bordering its southern edge was the only building of sorts, a long wooden covered portico housing a few tables, numerous benches, and several lecture podiums.

Many athletes, who were not competing in today's events or had completed their initial boxing and wrestling matches, were scattered about the grounds, stretching, running, jumping, or throwing this and that. There must have been at least fifty of them there, the air of fierce competitiveness replaced by a feeling of camaraderie. Four or five were splashing playfully in the stream on the other side of the gymnasium, and two young men were making water at the stream's far southern edge. Relaxing on benches under the portico were several elderly gentlemen, mentors and lovers of some of the young athletes, gesturing with possessive pride at their charges.

Mycrustes, one of Priene's burly minor athletes about my age, shouted to me and waved me over to him, where he was hefting several javelins, testing their weight and balance.

"Ho, Bias!" he greeted me with a grin. "Tell me which of these sticks you like best?" He tossed me one of the javelins. Now, I admit I am no Olympian athlete, but I do have a good strong right arm and can throw a mean javelin. I hefted each of the spears, finding its point of balance and comparing their weights.

"This one, I think." I tossed him the one that seemed right to me. He caught it nimbly and regarded its length with a suspicious eye.

"You think so? I thought perhaps that one with the yellow tip. I'm throwing in the initial rounds tomorrow morning you know, after the diaulos racing."

"The yellow-tip is certainly an excellent weapon," I hastened to assure him. "As a matter of fact, it was my other choice for the best one."

"I knew it was the right one." He grinned and tossed the yellow spear above his head. Catching it dexterously, he threw it in an easy spiral at a marker about forty paces away. Its shiny bronze point gleamed in the afternoon sunshine, before it plowed into the short grass.

"Have you seen Endemion about?" I glanced vaguely around the open area.

"Oh, yes, he's over there on the far side, practicing some long jumping with his admirers." He pointed toward a group of young men on the northern edge of the field, about two stades away. I thanked him and ambled over to Endemion's entourage.

There were a dozen young men clustered together, stretching, chatting, and laughing, apparently without a care in the world—no signs of the stress and tension of the competition. Here on the "cityless" grounds of the gymnasium they could be friendly comrades instead of serious rivals.

Endemion's face lit up when he spotted me coming, and he nudged a boy from Ephesus next to him.

"Hail, Bias, the mighty priest," he boomed. "Bless us with your wondrous presence." The other athletes grinned and winked, clearly delighted to be in his entourage.

"Hail, Endemion," I intoned with mock gravity, raising my hand in a benediction. "May you not fall on your gloriously large nose during the diaulos races tomorrow."

He howled and gave me a hug that set my bones creaking. I reflected wryly that I was getting enough bearhugs today to last for the rest of the year.

I noticed that Endemion and his fellows seemed to have no aversion to my black tunic, slapping me mightily on the back and jostling me with good-natured nudges. The memories of the young are very short.

"Gods, your hair looks like some drunken satyr has been at it. Who in Hades is your barber?"

"My illustrious mother," I managed with a grin. "So take care how you denigrate my superb coiffure." He howled again, and once more I received a tremendous hug. Disentangling my aching arms and chest, I asked if I could speak to him privately for a few moments. He readily assented, and we strolled to the stream's edge to rest our hot feet in its clear, pleasant coolness, while his friends went back to practice jumping.

"How goes your investigation of the death of Tyrestes?" Endemion inquired eagerly, his voice dropping to a whisper on the last few words.

"Very slowly. I just began this morning, remember?"

"I know you can find the murderer. You've always been a clever one!" His confidence touched me, his earnestness evident in his gaze. Was it possible that he admired me? How strange are the ways of the world, that the hope for Priene's glory should admire a lowly priest of Poseidon.

"Um, yes," I said. "You can be a great help in this matter, Endemion. You must tell me everything you can remember about the events of yesterday when you were with Tyrestes." His face fell a bit at this, and I reflected how like a child in many ways was this magnificent athlete. He sighed and paddled his feet in the water.

"Of course, noble Bias, I shall. Well, let me think. We marched the whole way from the city to the Panionion together, since the athletes from each city had their own section of the procession. Ah, it was grand, and Tyrestes was as happy as any of us! We wound our way through the hillocks over the top of Mount Mycale, and saw spread before us on the plain, all the people waiting to greet us, as if we were gods!"

He paused, and I could see his contentment and pride as he recalled every detail of each face he had looked upon in the adoring throng. He continued:

"We walked proudly down the mountainside to the altar site. Oh, it was fine—all those people shouting and waving! When we got to the altar, the wine girls who had proceeded us poured libations into the cups thrust upon us by the magistrates. Tyrestes and I were side by side the whole way. We took our cups eagerly to await the sacrificial toast. I remember Father gave Tyrestes and me each a cup, and the girls poured them full.

"Mine even overflowed onto my hand and wrist, and I remember laughing and winking at my pouring girl. How she laughed too—a plain young girl! But how her eyes sparkled!"

He paused again and glanced slyly at me.

"She was very firmly put together, if you know what I mean," he added, motioning with his hands in front of his chest. "And just about the right age where she's worth getting to know when her father's not around!"

"What happened next, Endemion?"

He rubbed the top of his curly head vigorously, and continued. "Well, let's see. We all stood waiting and listening to that bore Crystheus while he gave his speech to Poseidon, and then at the signal we quaffed our wine. I remember punching Tyrestes on the arm, and he grinned and squeezed my hand until it hurt. We turned back to watch the sacrifice, and the next thing I knew, I felt him sway against me and sink to the ground. I tried to hold him up, Bias, but it felt like he had no bones left! He just fell to the ground, and then vomited his wine onto my sandals! I could not hold him up!"

Endemion stopped abruptly, the swift flow of words cutting off sharply. He stared into the distance for a long moment, and then brought his gaze back to me.

"And then he died, didn't he, Bias?" he added softly. "You were there. He died. What could I have done?"

"Nothing, noble Endemion." I took him firmly by the arms and fixed his gaze with my own. "There was nothing you could do. There was nothing anyone could do!" He nodded sadly a few times, and looked away.

"That's all I remember," he concluded quietly. I wracked my brain for some further crumb of comfort I could give him, but nothing seemed to come.

"Endemion, my friend, did you see any action at the wine pouring that looked out of place? Something like someone placing powder or a liquid into a wine cup, or your pouring girl using one jug for you and a different one for Tyrestes?"

"No, I do not recall anything like that," he drawled, scratching his thick thatch of black curls again. "But, then again, everything was happening so fast. I don't think anybody could have poured anything into his wine cup. I was the closest person to him the whole time, and I think I would have noticed something like that, eh?"

I regarded him thoughtfully as he splashed his feet in the stream. Yes, indeed, he had been closest to Tyrestes the whole time, hadn't he? I spoke with what I hoped was deceptive innocence.

"How do you think Tyrestes would have fared in the games, if fate had not been so cruel as to cut him down?"

He stood up, took a few steps into the stream, and sat down abruptly in the running water, dashing it energetically into his face and hair. The drops of water dripping from his handsome head sparkled in the sunlight.

"He would have been very hard to beat. He was extremely good, you know, especially in the running races and pentathlon events."

"Do you think you could have beaten him?" I asked softly, staring directly into his eyes. His forehead creased with thought, and he smiled wryly.

"Yes, I think I would have beaten him," Endemion said in a tone as flat as the gymnasium grounds. "He was excellent, but I don't think his heart was really in these games. I believe that my endurance and persistence would have prevailed in the end." He rose out of the stream, shook himself, and clumped back to the water's edge. Removing the cloth swaddling his loins, he squeezed the liquid out of it and draped it around his shoulders to dry. We began walking back toward his admiring group of athletic friends.

"Why do you say that his heart was not in the competition?" I inquired curiously. "Surely to him as well as you, this is the chance of a lifetime for honor and fame."

"It is that, of course, " Endemion admitted easily enough, "but Tyrestes was troubled about things in his personal life lately. I don't really think it is something that we should talk about."

I halted abruptly, seized him by his muscular arm, and swung him around.

"We must talk about it," I said sharply. "This is not some sort of polite conversation, as you seem to think. I am attempting to find out who killed Tyrestes, remember? Now, I admit that I have never done anything like this before, but I believe that any information I can get about him might help to find his murderer." Startled, he murmured his answer.

"Well, then, of course. If you put it that way. Tyrestes was very concerned about his family and his estate. He confessed to me that he was not satisfied with that part of his life. It kept him from concentrating on his training."

"Did he tell you what was bothering him about his family life?"

"Not in so many direct words. But I know that he was left with many debts when his father, Tirachos, died several years ago. His estate was a small one, and he was looking for a way to increase his holdings." He stopped to observe one of his entourage try the long jump, frowning slightly when the leap proved to be a impressive one.

"How do you suppose he planned to enlarge his estate?" I already knew the answer to that question. Since all the land around the city-state of Priene was already owned, the only way one could increase one's landholding was in exchange for a debt or by marrying a woman with a land-heavy dowry. Since Endemion had said that Tyrestes was already in debt from his father's actions, he had to be searching for a prosperous bride.

"He was looking for a profitable marriage," Endemion said disdainfully. Well, he could sneer: his father Nolarion was one of the wealthiest and most powerful men in Priene.

"Any ideas on what families he may have been looking at?" We watched another of his comrades attempt the long jump. This one fell short of the last young man's leap, and Endemion smiled.

"I'm afraid I can't help you there," he answered. "I have no interest in things like that, and didn't really listen when he spoke about women, which he rarely did. Why should one worry about women with such fine young fellows as these here as companions?" He swept his arm to cover the gymnasium area as he spoke.

"One final question," I said. "Do you know if he had any feuds or problems with any of the other athletes here at the games?"

Endemion shook his head. "Oh, no, nothing like that. He was very well liked, you know. Why, even these fellows around me now would be clustered around him if he were still alive." His voice trailed off wistfully at this last admission, and he turned away to begin stretching for a run. I could discern no bitterness in his tone, but what kind of expert am I?

"Yes, well, thank you for the information," I said heartily and clapped him on the shoulder. I turned also, and began to stroll back toward the city's houses, when he spoke from behind me.

"Bias, one question that you asked. I just remembered it. If it's any help, we weren't poured wine by the same girl at the altar ceremony. As I said, mine was a plain girl with an impressive chest. His pourer was quite beautiful, as I recall, but didn't smile much. Not the same girl at all."

CHAPTER X

DISPIRITED, I MADE MY way back home. My conversation with Endemion had only added to the list of things I now needed to consider. Thoughts spun through my mind like so many seabirds darting after fish on the sea's surface, as I strode back through the city and towards the west, where my family would be preparing for the dorpon evening meal. The sun was close to setting, lengthening the shadows of the olive trees gnarled branches, as I turned up the path that led from the main road to my father's estate.

What information had I gotten from Endemion? Tyrestes was not fully concentrating on the great games, held only once every four years, because he was worried about his family and his estate's debts. He needed money or more land to pay those debts left by his father, and one clear way to get that was to marry well, or at least to marry rich. He had been Priene's premier athlete, our best hope for winning the Panionic Games, despite Endemion's assurances that he could have beaten him. He and Endemion had both received their cups at the altar ceremony from Nolarion, but had been offered wine by different pouring girls. According to Endemion, who admitted he had been swept up in the swift excitement of the proceedings,

Tyrestes' pourer had been beautiful, while Endemion's had been plain with an impressive chest and sparkling eyes! I have to admit that my prejudiced viewpoint assigned Ossadia as his pourer and Bilassa as Tyrestes' wine girl, but I had been there myself, and had observed many plain and pretty girls pouring away incessantly for the hundred athletes and the crowd of spectators. And all that information depended on whether or not Endemion was telling the truth! I had noted the edge of envy in his voice, when he admitted that the fickle minor athletes forming his entourage would have clustered around the personable Tyrestes, if the latter had still been alive.

Entering our family manor house through the prodomus, I walked down the central hallway and out the back to the small courtyard. Sure enough, my father, mother, and six sisters were all out there, listening to Holicius expound on the importance of the day's events. The girls exhibited various levels of interest in his pronouncements, but I noted with pride that my mother was watching him unceasingly, seeming to hang on his every word. My mother knew how to keep her family, and especially her husband, happy, healthy, and contented. Since men did not normally wed for love, a woman who could develop and keep the love of a man was a rare person indeed. Yet my mother seemed to do it effortlessly, even though I knew that she worked tirelessly at it.

My father paused while the three younger girls hurled themselves bodily upon me. I alternately hugged and fended them off as I dragged myself over to his bench, dragged being the proper word since Tapho had wrapped herself around my left leg and was hanging on for dear life. I tickled her under her arms, until she broke off and ran shrieking away, followed with laughter and further shrieks by the other two.

Holicius and Tesessa both rose and embraced me, after I had freed myself from the small harpies. On a bench to the left sat Arlana and Risalla, one at each end like birds on opposite ends of a clothesline. I could almost feel the tension between them like an invisible wall, and sighed, returning my mother's hug. Ulania, as usual, would be supervising Selcra as she prepared dorpon for the family.

"My son, I was just explaining the intricacies involved in a good wrestling match," Holicius said enthusiastically, settling himself again on his bench. My mother smiled at me, and gently took one of his hands, as she turned back to him. I plopped down on the bench on his other side, and gave him my attention.

As he spoke, his head swivelled back and forth from me to my mother like a door on a hinge. "As I was saying, the superior wrestler is not necessarily the stronger one, but is more likely to be the cleverer one. You saw how Endemion won his match today as compared to Krelonan?" I nodded.

"Well, then, you saw the two different techniques in action! Endemion's knowledge of footwork and leverage won him his match, while Krelonan used brute strength."

"But, Father," I protested mildly, "you just admitted that both wrestlers won their bouts."

"Indeed, yes." He nodded vigorously and gave his beard a gentle tug. "However, I think you will find that in the matches to come, Krelonan may run into problems, if he is matched to a large young man who knows how to use another's clumsy strength to his own advantage." I tried to imagine the hulking Krelonan losing to a lithe competitor, but the picture seemed ludicrous. On the other hand, I had witnessed many wrestling matches myself, and it was true that you simply could not tell by size or strength alone who would be victorious.

"What about the pancration, though?" I asked. This bloody contest, a favorite among the lower classes and admittedly gaining popularity among many of the aristocrats, was wrestling combined with every dirty trick in the book. The contestants began the match on their feet, but unlike wrestling, where the action stopped if any part of the body above the knee touched the ground, the pancration continued on the ground, until one of the athletes surrendered. Almost anything was allowed, including punching, kicking, and strangling. I had never been fond of watching this "sport." Neither, apparently, had my father.

"Pancration is not a true sport," he said scornfully, "and should never have been allowed in the games. It's simply a sop to the mob's thirst for blood! But I will grant you that brute strength is vital to win it! Krelonan should do very well indeed in that contest."

After a few more minutes of discussion, Selcra announced that the dorpon was ready. My father and I retired to the andron in the front of the house to lie on our klines, and the women went to the gynaikonitis rooms in the rear. This evening's repast was a light one, but very tasty, I must say. We dined on mackerel pickled with olive oil, vinegar, dill, and fennel, and nibbled horta, a green leafy vegetable served with olive oil and vinegar. To offset the sour taste, Selcra had baked fresh maza bread and included several new onions to munch. Holicius topped it off by treating us to several kylixes of his best wine from Chios, as a sort of celebration of the first day of the games. It makes my mouth water just to remember it!

At the meal's end my father announced that he was tired after such an exciting day, and wanted to get up early tomorrow to watch the initial bouts of diaulos running and javelin throwing at the stadium, and then proceed from there to the hippodrome to view the chariot-racing. We did not have a chariot entered for these games, which Holicius greatly regretted, since the owner of the winning chariot and not the charioteer, was the person who gained the most laurels. Nevertheless, he apparently did not intend to let this lack of personal ownership deter him from cheering on his friends' entries (and perhaps indulge in a few small bets on the side?).

After my father retired to his sleeping room, I sauntered back out to the courtyard and sought out Duryattes, finding him enjoying his own dorpon in his family's small quarters against the back wall. He grinned as I stood at the door, and took a monstrous bite from a huge onion he clutched in a grimy fist.

"Greetings, young master." He leapt to his feet and bowed his head toward me. I motioned for him to follow me outside into the courtyard, and nodded courteously at Dryses and Selcra, who returned the salutation, and resumed eating their meal. Duryattes brought his onion with him, and snatched a hunk of maza from a shelf as we left.

I eyed him irritably as we seated ourselves on a bench, and he alternately stuffed his mouth with bread and onion. When he had finished both, he stared back at me and wiped a hand over his mouth.

"Well?" I asked impatiently.

"Well what, master?" he inquired innocently. I felt the hackles beginning to rise on the back of my neck, and he must have sensed it too, because he immediately stopped teasing and launched into his tale of adventure in the city of Priene.

"When we parted at the city gate, I walked to the agora right away. You should have been there, master! I have never seen more people in one place at one time. The market place was packed full, not just with slaves buying food and wine for their masters at the games, but with all types and varieties of visitors from near and far. Why, there were some people there that I could hardly understand, their accents were so thick! I know they were speaking Greek because I recognized a word now and then, but their accents were barbaric!" Despite my annoyance at his impertinence, I had to hide a smile at this, since it was clear that to him if one spoke in any accent other than that of Priene, one was a barbarian. And this was even though he was Carian, not Ionian!

"How did you go about trying to find the information we wanted?" I asked curiously, caught by his sense of excitement. He puffed out his thin chest.

"Just strolled about using the old ears, eh, young master? The main topic of conversation was the games themselves, you see, but now and then other subjects came up, like the price of wine or meat or olives. Master, you should have heard what the wine sellers are charging for a kylix of watered local wine! Not even Chios, but just local! It was scandalous, but the visitors were buying it up like it was going to turn into donkey urine tomorrow." He shook his head in worldly consternation. I bit back an impatient comment or two.

"And did you find out anything that may help us solve this mystery?"

He glanced at me noting the *us* in my question.

"Well, master, let me tell you, it wasn't easy. I would have thought that Tyrestes' death would have been the subject of conversation, but this was not so! It was almost as if the people were avoiding talking about it. As if merely talking about it would bring bad luck. I wandered about until I came across several slaves talking about religious ceremonies, and was able with a few well-turned phrases to lead them onto the subject of the altar ceremony." The young man preened himself like a bird with gorgeous plumage, and again I had to hide a smile.

"Let me tell you, master," he said again, "they had more theories about Tyrestes' death than a sophist. I listened to everything from Poseidon's anger with Tyrestes to Apollo's jealousy of him to the revenge of certain ladies he had toyed with. Once I got a couple of them going on the subject, more people joined in until a whole section of the market was buzzing about what caused his death." This was more like it. This was what I needed.

"Did you find out if anybody saw anything?"

"Mostly, they chattered about every piece of gossip under the sun." Duryattes sighed. "I don't think anybody saw anything directly, if you know what I mean." I knew what he meant. He had not found a witness to the actual scene at the ceremony, a witness who might be able to cast some light on an increasingly murky situation. I cursed under my breath. How could this whole episode have happened in public without anyone noticing anything?

"But I did find out some gossip that may be important to you," the young slave continued after a moment. He fidgeted on the bench for a moment, and then jumped to his feet, unable to sit still for another heartbeat.

"A slave from the family of Kreton was in the group, and he told us that Tyrestes had visited their estate several times in the past month. According to some talk this slave had overheard between the mistress of the house and Kreton's only daughter, Tyrestes was interested in a possible match between himself and the daughter to unite the families. He said that the mother initially was in favor of the idea and the daughter was doubtful, but that later, their roles reversed!"

"What do you mean, their roles reversed?" Duryattes was pacing up and down in front of the bench now.

"Kreton's slave said that the daughter later seemed much more open to the idea of a match, but the mother discouraged it. He mentioned that the mother had discovered that Tyrestes was apparently seeing Valato with the same intention for Valato's daughter. The whole thing was muddled, you see, since Tyrestes had no father or mother to make a match for him, and had to kind of stumble along himself. Kreton's daughter seemed quite shocked that Tyrestes was seeing this other girl, Ossadia, I believe her name is, and burst into tears while she was talking with her mother. The mother took this as a sign that the daughter had an unhealthy interest in Tyrestes, and forbade her to speak any more about him."

"Was the daughter's name Bilassa?" I asked eagerly, overjoyed to get some significant information from the boy at last.

"Yes, I believe it was, young master! Bilassa, the daughter of Kreton."

"Well, done, Duryattes. That gives me another avenue to explore that may bear fruit!"

"Wait, master, that is not all I found," he continued importantly. "Speaking about bearing fruit, figuratively, that is." He looked at me sideways and rewarded me with a broad wink.

"What else?"

"With Kreton's older male slave was his daughter. Let me tell you, she was a pretty little thing. Anyway, she added to the conversation as well, although she nearly got a slap from her father for her troubles." Duryattes' look now could only be described as sly and knowing.

"The people around Kreton's slave were chewing on this information, when the girl piped up that she knew that Tyrestes and Bilassa had done more than just talk about the future.

"The father asked her what she meant. 'Well, Father,' she said, 'I know that they were playing the two-backed beast during his visit before the mistress soured on him.' The father asked how she knew this, and she said, 'Well, Father, I'm a woman, I wait upon the young mistress, and I can tell these things, you know.' That is what nearly earned her the slap in the face. Her father's hand missed her only by a fraction, and she immediately humbly begged his forgiveness!"

"Are you saying that Tyrestes and Bilassa slept together?" I asked, stunned that this kind of gossip should be floating about the bazaar. Although it was not uncommon for an unloved wife to have an affair with an attractive young male, for a unwed girl to succumb to such a temptation could be disastrous for her marriage prospects. Even the rumor of such a thing could easily deter suitors in search of a virgin bride.

"That is the word at the marketplace, master." He threw himself back onto the bench and looked at me expectantly.

"If that's the case, and I am not saying it is," I amended hurriedly, "then that would certainly explain Bilassa's distress at hearing from her mother that Tyrestes might be pursuing Ossadia as well as herself." I thought for a moment, while Duryattes stared at me eagerly.

"She certainly would not have told anybody in her family," I mused, almost to myself. "That would ruin her for sure. But Risalla said that before the ceremonial procession Bilassa acted as if she knew what she was talking about when it came to lovemaking. Would that be a reason for Bilassa to poison Tyrestes, thinking that she would not be wedded to him, or maybe to anybody? No, that's ridiculous! She still would have been in the running, so to speak, for the place at his side as his wife. Yet she may well have spoken to Ossadia before the procession, and the gods above only know what that one would have told her. It would be possible to obtain the poison hellebore at a short notice — it is very common as a medicine, I believe that physician said yesterday." I turned back to Duryattes.

"We know that Bilassa was one of the pouring girls," I said slowly. "Were you able to find out who she poured wine for at the altar ceremony?"

"No, young master. Remember, I said this was all gossip, not eyewitness accounts of the ceremony itself. The ceremony was for citizens, after all, and only a few serving slaves had been there."

The sun had gone down now, and there was a slight nip in the late spring air. The only light came from a small olive oil lamp that Dryses had lit at the far end of the courtyard. Duryattes hugged his thin tunic about himself.

"Is that all, master?" he asked, clearly anxious to go to his warm cot.

"Yes, that is all, Duryattes. You have done extremely well. I won't hesitate to call on you again if I need more information." He got up, stretched and yawned, and started back toward his hut. Then he stopped abruptly, turned, and walked slowly back to me.

"Master, there is something else I picked up at the agora," he confided after a slight hesitation. "I am not sure it has anything to do with this matter, but it is something you should know for our family's sake."

"What are you talking about?" I had heard enough for one day, and longed for my bed as well.

"I found out that the noble Tyrestes had one further problem to complicate his life. Not only was he searching for a bride with a dowry, he was searching for one for his brother Usthius as well. Although he's not old enough to wed, the noble Usthius is old enough to become betrothed and thereby further enhance their family fortunes." He hesitated again.

"Yes, go on," I urged him, fascinated despite my weariness. A bride for Usthius as well!

"I was told that Tyrestes and Usthius did not get along together at all. Usthius apparently had no desire to become betrothed to any female chosen by Tyrestes, but wanted to choose one himself and then have Tyrestes arrange the engagement. I have heard that Usthius had one in mind, but that Tyrestes did not feel that she had enough money. I have also heard that Usthius was at the altar ceremony, off to one side out of sight. Of course, with all the excitement and confusion at the time, would it have been possible for Usthius to tamper with some wine or a cup? And the girl was there too, the girl that Tyrestes would not consider." Duryattes stopped again, and looked at me imploringly.

"What are you trying to say, Duryattes? What does this have to do with our family?"

The young slave visibly swallowed, gathered his courage, and blurted out. "Young master, the girl that Usthius wants to wed is your sister Risalla!"

CHAPTER XI

As you can probably imagine, I did not sleep particularly well with this bit of indigestible information about Risalla and Usthius sticking in my craw like a piece of bad meat. I tossed and turned on my cot all night with visions of them all—Bilassa, Ossadia, Nolarion, Valato, Krelonan, Kreton, and Endemion—whirling through my mind, pieces of some strange puzzle that I needed to solve, but did not know where to begin.

I could not remember much about these thoughts in the morning, but one curious and repulsive scene was left there, no doubt gleefully by Morpheus, the god of dreams.

I was seated on the top of the small shrine of Apollo on the northern edge of Priene's gymnasium area, but instead of being surrounded by the small sacred olive grove, the surface of a restless sea spread out behind me as far as the eye could reach.

The waves of the sea were gray and spume-tossed, and I could feel the spray soaking the back of my tunic. Before me on the gymnasium grounds many people were practicing various sports events, and I let my gaze wander, seemingly not at all surprised at the various odd encounters I saw. Nolarion, Tyrestes, Risalla, and the Miletian athlete Habiliates were throwing javelins to my left; Endemion, Bilassa, and Usthius sprinted down the field in a race to my right; and in the center of my field of vision Valato and his daughter, Ossadia, were passionately kissing, while Euphemius and Kreton sprinkled them with hundreds of flower petals. Beyond them, spread out like a gigantic multicolored cloth upon the ground, the crowd cheered and swayed. Oddly enough, even though I had never met Bilassa or Usthius, I know they were there in that dream.

Tyrestes and Habiliates tossed their javelins far down the field, while Risalla leaned against hers and solemnly stared back at me. The magistrate Nolarion suddenly whirled about from his throwing position and hurled his javelin at the crowd. It struck somebody deep in the throng—I could not see who— but this simply caused the people to break out in renewed cheering and screaming. Nolarion was beaming back at them with his hands held high in the air, when he was felled by a tremendous blow from behind by the Miletian athlete, Habiliates. This met with triumphant approval from Ossadia, who pushed her father away and ran to throw herself into the Miletian's waiting arms. Usthius, who had won his race against a panting Bilassa and strangely lethargic Endemion, completed his run by snatching up Risalla over his shoulder as he sprinted by and flinging her javelin into the back of Tyrestes, who was now wrestling with the risen Nolarion. The spear protruding from his back did not seem to bother him much, but he could not reach it with his searching hands, so Habiliates, with Ossadia twined about him, plucked it from the bunched muscles and tossed it contemptuously aside. Obviously infuriated by this,

Nolarion and Bilassa began arguing about who owned the javelin, Nolarion emphasizing his points by tearing great hunks of his beard away and tossing them at the beautiful girl. Throughout Euphemius and Kreton strolled about, throwing petals to the wind, while Endemion stared stupidly at the crowd.

I had a banging headache when I awoke, and fervently wished that Hypnos, the god of sleep, would keep a firmer hand on his son Morpheus. I am well aware that dreams are messages sent by this fickle god, but if you can decipher that one, then you, and not I, should be the priest of Poseidon.

At any rate I did not have the chance to question Risalla alone about her possible dalliance with the now independent Usthius, because the family breakfasted hurriedly and, with quick strides that caused my younger sisters to protest, walked back to the city to try and catch the opening diaulos, double-length races at the stadium. There were even more spectators than the day before. They were cheering and screaming at the various racers, who grinned and bobbed like olives in a tub of water. Gods, there must have been 8000 people packing the stadium, and the cloths and cushions they used to ease the discomfort of sitting on the rock-cut grandstand seats would have covered the flat stadium grounds several times over. Even at this early hour of the morning the wine and food sellers were doing a roaring trade and revelling in every hard-fought moment of it.

One of the opening heats in the diaulus races commenced just as we arrived, fighting our way down to our places in the lower part of the central stands. Thanks be to Poseidon, the aristocratic citizens of Priene had permanent seats in this best part of the structure. Otherwise, we certainly would not have been able to get close to the athletic contests. Even so, if we had arrived a little later, we would no doubt have found our places taken by screeching spectators daring us to remove them bodily!

In the diaulus race the contestants sprint down the entire length of the field, curve around a pole set at the far end, and then bound back to the starting line. The trick is to balance the need for great speed in the first half of the race against the ability to turn around in the least possible time without touching either the far wall or the pole.

Habiliates of Miletus was in the heat we viewed as we arrived, and won easily, almost jogging past the finish line, a lazy smile on his handsome face. The audience, filled with visitors from his great city across the bay, erupted into wild screams and cheers as their hero strutted about, his fists raised high and his head thrown back, basking in the accolades. The sound pounded against the stadium walls like storm waves against a rocky shore. I thought that he was easily the fastest runner I had ever seen, and if anybody could beat him, the winner would certainly have earned his laurel wreath.

My father glanced disdainfully at the screaming Miletians all around us, and cupping a hand round his mouth, bawled into my ear. "This is a good example of how a mob attitude can overcome even the most sensitive of men. I know there are citizens of good repute in this crowd of Miletians. I have met many of them. And yet, here they are howling like so many wolves in the woods!"

I had seen Holicius shrieking with the wildest of them when an athlete from Priene won an event, so his comment seemed one-sided at best. But he was my father, so I nodded vigorously and turned my attention back to the contests.

Several more heats were run before I saw my chance to talk to Risalla alone.

My mother mentioned that she would welcome a snack of some maza and olives, and I leaped to my feet, hauling up Risalla with me by her firm rounded arm.

"We will get you and the girls some food, Mother," I volunteered enthusiastically. "Father, would you like some wine?" Holicius nodded distractedly, his gaze fixed on the Priene entry for the next heat. Tesessa smiled at me and my sister, and waved us away.

"What are you doing? I want to watch the races!" protested Risalla, as I pulled her along toward a food seller near one of the stadium tunnel exits. As I had done with Ossadia the day before, I stopped in the tunnel to speak out of immediate range of the roaring crowd. Risalla sensed something was up; her eyes were wary.

"What in Hades do you think you are playing at with Usthius?" I threw at her, hoping to catch her off guard. As I have indicated, Risalla would never be able to build a temple or write poetry, but I respected her resourcefulness. I hoped the blunt approach was the wisest one in this case.

She caught her breath, held it for a moment, and then let it out in a slow sigh. I imagined that I could actually see her thoughts racing as she considered me in silence.

"And who is this Usthius?" she asked softly after a heartbeat or two, looking directly up at me.

"You know perfectly well who he is!" I shot back at her. "He is the brother of Tyrestes, and is now the head of that family, the heir to its land and fortune, limited though that may be!" She regarded me as if I were some strange, smelly kind of fish, and turned away to watch the race from the mouth of the tunnel.

"Father does not permit me to talk to men without his permission. You know that. When would I have had the chance to *play at* anything with this Usthius? I am never out of sight of one of the family, am I?" She glanced back at me with a smile. She is getting to be very good at this, particularly at her age, I thought. It is amazing what you do not really know about people close to you, until some unforeseen event occurs to trigger shifts in feeling and awareness.

"Don't dissemble with me, Risalla! I have a witness who saw you with him at the altar ceremony the day before yesterday—the ceremony where you were so busy pouring wine that you didn't notice anything unusual!"

Her lips clamped together in anger, drawing her mouth into a sharp line. What had happened to my little sister of the rosy cheeks and cheery smile? Now she seemed like some changeling substituted by a mischievous nymph. I heard the breath hiss into her throat, as she drew it past clenched teeth.

"Your witness is mistaken, Bias. I have heard of the name, Usthius, now that you have reminded me who he is. But I have never met him. Again, how could I? And what would the head of a family want with me? I'm not old enough to wed or even to dally with."

"To *dally with*?" I repeated in a sharp tone. "Where do you get these ideas? My witness is not mistaken. Apparently this is common gossip all over the agora, as if you were some common slut! Usthius is considering choosing you to be his wife, and asked Tyrestes to look into the possibility of a betrothal. But Tyrestes did not think you would bring a large enough dowry to help pay off his family debts! Does all this sound familiar?"

Risalla's eyes darted back and forth; she moistened her lips nervously.

"None of that is true," she said. "I may have met this Usthius at the Panionion for a moment or perhaps seen him in the city when I was there shopping with Ulania or Mother, but he certainly never showed any romantic interest in me. I believe I would have recognized that, even as young as I am!"

I am certain of that myself, I thought, as I remembered the hungry way in which she had stared at the wrestlers yesterday. Oh, yes, sister, I am positive you would recognize *romantic interest.*

"So now you admit that you have met Usthius several times, including at the altar ceremony?" I persisted.

"So what if I did? I have done nothing improper. Can I be held responsible for baseless rumors in the marketplace?"

"Let me spell it out for you, sister, since you're having difficulty seeing the obvious, even if you are finally telling the truth. Usthius was interested in a possible betrothal to you, but Tyrestes needed large dowries to pull his family estate out of debt. Our father can afford to present you with only a modest dowry, but enough of one for a man interested in allying himself with the house of Holicius. Usthius was the second son of his family. With Tyrestes dead he would become the family heir and could wed whomever he wished. You were a wine pouring girl for the athletes at the ceremony, which would include his brother Tyrestes. How hard could it be in the excitement for him to make sure a certain cup, a special cup, was given to his brother? And how much easier would this have been if a certain wine pouring girl made sure that Tyrestes got that cup?" I drew a deep breath, watching her closely.

Risalla was shocked, there was no denying that. Her eyes had widened, and the pupils had grown large and dark with surprise. I could see white all around them. Her hands were twined tightly together in front of her chiton. She shook her head violently in denial.

"No, I never!" she cried. "I never did anything like that! Bias, it's not true! How can you even think that of your own sister?"

"Then tell me the truth," I demanded harshly, grasping her upper arms in my hands and squeezing hard. Her flesh bulged around the outsides of my fists, and she winced in pain. "Tell me what you know about Usthius!"

"I don't know anything! Please, Bias, let me sit down. Let me sit down." I guided her to a large rock outside the stadium entrance tunnel, and she sank down upon it. I am sure Mother is wondering what happened to her snack, I thought illogically for a moment.

"Tell me what you know about Usthius and anything he said to you," I said more quietly, crouching down beside her, and taking her face in my hands. The tears were tumbling out of her eyes now, sliding down her face, and plopping from her chin onto the breast of her chiton. But she wept silently. I waited until the river had dried up, and she looked up at me miserably.

"Usthius did say he was interested in me, both before in the city and at the ceremony," she gulped, rubbing her reddened nose and dabbing at her eyes with her sleeve. "I saw him in Priene twice when Mother sent me on some errands, while she was shopping. We met the first time when I bought some fish at the stand near the theater. Mother scolded me terribly right in public when I didn't come back to her for half an hour."

"And the next time?"

"The next time was at one of the fruit stalls in the agora. I know it was not right to talk to him, but he stood just out of sight of Mother around a corner, and we talked for a half hour or so. It was then he told me he was looking for a bride, and that he knew about me and my family. He claimed he had great respect for Father, and that he planned to bring up the matter with his older brother Tyrestes, who was the head of his family. Oh, Bias, I listened to him and laughed, but I didn't think he was serious. Men are not supposed to pick their own wives, I know that. I just thought he was trying to . . . you know, soften me up for some later meeting, where he would try to make love to me."

She was so calm and matter-of-fact that I wondered where she had learned about these things. I was sure it was not from Tesessa. My mother was loving to all her daughters, but quite old-fashioned when it came to discussing such things as love-making. Why, I had seen her blush when my father talked about the mating of horses or donkeys!

"I didn't think any more about the subject or him until I saw him at the altar ceremony," Risalla continued, her tears now dried and defiance stealing with soft footfalls back into her voice. I could have slapped her, but my mother would have come after me with a kitchen knife if I did anything like that. So I remained silent and tried to look stern.

"What happened at the ceremony? How did you have time to speak to him with all the marching and pouring and so forth?"

"He popped out of the crowd just as I walked away from Mother and Father. A lot of young men walked with the girls in the procession from that point to the altar hill, trying to show off in front us to draw our attention from the athletes, who looked so splendid. I don't think anybody thought it was odd that one of them walked with me."

Perhaps not odd, I thought, but plenty of people had noticed, as Duryattes found out in the agora yesterday.

"What did he say at the ceremony?" I asked. Risalla hesitated.

"Get on with it," I growled. She sniffed, and slumped back dejectedly on her rock.

"He babbled something about Tyrestes standing in the way of our betrothal, and how if his brother were to die, he would be the heir and could choose whomever he wished for a bride. I am afraid that I just laughed; I didn't say a word."

She paused. "He is such a boy, Bias, especially compared to the athletes here for the games. He looked at me very oddly, I remember, and said again that he could be head of his family if Tyrestes met with an accident. I think I annoyed him by laughing at him, because he stormed away. That was the last I saw of him. Things got so hectic that I didn't have time for anything except pouring and fending off the hands of the athletes around me."

Risalla looked very satisfied with this memory, and smoothed her chiton over her upper body, running her hands over herself.

By the gods, I thought, she might as well wear a sign that says, Take Me To The Nearest Bushes, I Am Yours. But I did believe she was telling the truth, for all that.

"You're sure that's all? You didn't see him next to or behind the cups and wine amphoras, by chance?"

"No, I did not see him, but that doesn't mean he wasn't there. There were several young men who were handing cups quickly to the magistrates, who gave them then to each athlete with a quick blessing."

"What did you just say?" I asked softly, peering intently at her.

"I said that some young men were giving the cups to the magistrates, who handed them to the athletes," she repeated impatiently. "Then we girls would pour the wine into the cups, while we were trying to keep from being pawed."

"Just a moment. I recall seeing the magistrates giving full wine cups to the athletes, not empty ones for you to fill." I tried to remember the exact sequence of that part of the ritual.

"Well, yes, at first," Risalla said irritably. "But that was so slow and there were so many athletes and other citizens demanding a ceremonial kylix, that after a few minutes the magistrates began thrusting empty cups at the contestants, and we moved among them, pouring wine into their outthrust kylixes. You saw what happened with Crystheus and the ox."

Of course, I thought. In the confusion it would have been simple for Usthius to hand the magistrate Nolarion a poisoned cup, when it was Tyrestes' turn to receive a kylix. Even if he saw it, Tyrestes would have simply thought it was Usthius joining the celebration. Usthius could have poisoned his brother, just as Bilassa could have poisoned her lover, or Endemion could have poisoned his chief rival.

"Yes, he could have done it!" I muttered, staring at Risalla. She looked startled, and then shook her head emphatically.

"Do you mean Usthius could have poisoned Tyrestes? No, Bias, he could not have done that. He *is* such a boy, after all!"

CHAPTER XII

THE SOLE EVENT SCHEDULED in the games that afternoon was the chariot race.

This was held at the hippodrome, a large outdoor structure located to the east of Priene's gymnasium field and slightly lower down the slope of Mount Mycale. Actually, it was not a structure at all, having no seats, no beams, and no roof: it was simply a wide oval track about five stades in circumference surrounded by a low stone wall, approximately chest high and designed to keep the careening chariots from bounding outside the track and smashing into the watching spectators, who held a reasonable belief that they would not be crushed by runaway horses and carts. The track was broad enough to allow six chariots to race neck and neck down its straight sides, but of course they could and very often did get hopelessly tangled at the ends of the oval.

The crowd could choose a number of ways in which to view the action. Those who arrived very early (often the day before the races) could sit on the wall, dangling their legs over the edge and daring the charioteers to clip them off. This sometimes did happen, which caused the magistrates to frown on this practice, popular as it was among the bold young segments of the population. A safer and easier way to watch, was to arrive at the hippodrome just as early, but to stand close behind the wall. I always thought the best way was to rent a seat in the makeshift stands invariably set up by enterprising citizens the morning of the contest. Being made of whatever pieces of wood, beams, and rope the builder could come up with, these rickety structures could and occasionally did collapse in the midst of a particularly dramatic race, but on the whole, afforded one a relatively safe vantage point from which to cheer and hiss. Of course, the builders charged an arm and a leg for a good seat, but what was one to do when one wanted to see the clash of horses, frail wooden conveyances, and straining drivers? One paid.

And so the family dutifully followed my father, who dutifully followed the throng, which enthusiastically made its way from the stadium to the hippodrome in the early afternoon. Unlike the foot races, wrestling, and boxing, the chariot racing and the horse racing (scheduled for the next day), were single events that occurred only once during the course of the games. All the glory and honor to be earned by winning these events had to be accomplished in one mighty effort of skill compounded with luck. The charioteer who walked away with the crown of laurel leaves earned eternal fame for himself and particularly for his horses' owner, for the owner was the person who received the lion's share of accolades. You see, we Ionians—and the mainland Greeks as well—tended to believe it was the horses who strove the most to win the race, rather than the charioteer. Therefore the horses' owner and trainer were given the greater share of the glory. But don't feel sorry for the charioteer—after all, a winner is a winner in any case.

Holicius, being of sound mind and deep enough purse, had already rented bleacher seats for us the day before the race. As I have mentioned, chariot racing was one of his favorites, and I believe he would have sold one of my sisters for a good seat at the hippodrome. But all the way over to the site he grumbled unceasingly about the outrageous price of a seat in the stands, compared to what it was when he was a boy.

The sun burned down relentlessly from a cloudless bright blue sky, and the sweating, jostling herd of humanity filled the racing grounds to overflowing, until it seemed that the fields would start spitting people out like seeds from an overripe grape. We fought our way through to the stands of Amphodias the carpenter, who was standing guard over his bleachers like Jason defending the fabled golden fleece. As we approached, Amphodias was snarling at a desperate spectator who was trying to hand him a mina coin.

"No, I have no seats left," he shouted, staring longingly at the mina, which was worth sixty stater, more than he normally earned in a week. But he tore his gaze away and bestowed an ingratiating smile on my father.

"Noble Holicius, welcome to my stands! I have your seats awaiting you here. There they are, just there, at the very top, just as you ordered." He pointed toward a plank set at the top of the bleachers, conspicuously unoccupied.

"Hey, I wanted to buy those seats," complained the man with the mina. "You can't just sell them to him. I was here first!" The carpenter, his hard hands balled into fists, whirled on the protester, who shrank back in surprise.

"This is the noble Holicius, an aristocrat of Priene," Amphodias yelled. "He bought his seats days ago! I have nothing left!" The complainer slunk away, muttering about the inequities of *democracy* in this rat-infested city-state. The carpenter turned back toward my father, who was doing his best to hold himself straight and appear above it all.

"This way, this way, noble Holicius." He gestured toward the empty seats. "I see you have your beautiful family with you, sir." He reached for my mother's arm, and pulled back as she transfixed him with an icy stare. We climbed over several fellow citizens to the top of the stands. Holicius stood, looking down into the hippodrome.

"I suppose this will have to do," he fussed. "I was hoping for better seats, but we were lucky to get these." Tesessa patted his hand, and my sisters tumbled over one another in their haste to get the *best* seat. When they all were properly in place, my father looked them over carefully one by one. After all, it was very unusual for wives and daughters to be displayed in public, and I think he was at a loss as to how they should look. Ulania was with us today, balancing a golden Elissa on her knees as she squinted nearsightedly around her. As usual Arlana and Risalla sat at opposite ends of the plank, the former gazing disinterestedly about, while the latter meticulously inspected her fingernails, studiously ignoring both Arlana and me. Tirah and Tapho perched between my father and mother, excitedly bouncing up and down as they chattered away to each other. I bowed to Tesessa and addressed Holicius.

"Father, if you will pardon me, I need to seek out and speak to several people about my *task*." After a long moment, he waved me away to go about my business.

Climbing down from the stands, I strolled about searching the crowd for familiar faces. The throng was like an everchanging and multicolored fresco, flowing around and between the sets of stands and rebounding from the hippodrome walls like insects bouncing off a thin cloth screen. I had an idea where to find the person I was looking for, as the aristocrats were sure to be in the best seats. I had also unleashed Duryattes again, and just for an instant spotted him circulating among the slaves waiting to attend to their masters in the bleachers. I spied Valato and his family, including the bored-looking Ossadia, sitting off to my right in another set of stands. For a moment her eyes locked onto mine; she smiled a small, secret smile, and then looked away toward the track.

A deafening roar from the waiting army of onlookers announced the spectacle of the animal tenders beginning to lead the teams of horses onto the track from a side entrance. Not yet harnessed to their chariots, the horses were able to prance about, snorting and biting at the harassed slaves attempting to jockey them into position. Already on the hippodrome floor the chariots were waiting for their chargers, their position having been predetermined by lot. The charioteers and owners had not made their entrance onto the stage yet, but that would follow when the handlers had hooked the groups of four impatient animals to each of the waiting carts. Above it all I could hear the hawkers entreating the people to buy maza, wine, and olives.

I purchased a cheap kylix of watered wine, swallowed it quickly, grimacing at its sour taste, and moved on to spy Nolarion talking earnestly to Endemion near the competitor's entrance.

I could not make out what the magistrate was saying to his son, but I saw the young man nod with a grim expression and head to the holding area, where the drivers and owners were gathering. I quickly strode over to Nolarion and caught his attention with a wave. He grimaced as he recognized me, and then smiled in welcome.

"Good day, Bias," he boomed, a grin splitting his great black beard. "I was just giving my son my final pointers on handling his horses. Not that he needs any, of course!"

"Sir, I have discovered something of possible interest in the wine ceremony at the Panionion." I cupped my hand around my mouth to be heard above the steady roar of the crowd. "May I ask you a question about the pouring that day?" With an expression of patient suffering and a deep sigh, he indicated that I should continue.

"Sir, I have been informed that the magistrates did not necessarily take the kylix cups from the tables themselves to hand to athletes for the pouring of the wine, but that in some cases, young men passed the cups from the tables to you in the crush of the crowd!"

Nolarion's expression changed from forbearance to interest.

"Magistrate, do you remember if this happened? Did you always take a kylix from the table nearby or were they passed to you?" His gnarled right hand reached up to stroke the luxurious beard.

"Well, I don't know," he admitted slowly. "I suppose that . . . wait. Yes, I remember now. Yes, I believe I did have a young man behind me passing cups to me. Yes, perhaps after the pouring got very busy. There were a lot of athletes there, you know, and then many citizens wanted a cup too. Perhaps somebody did pass cups to me and the other magistrates!" He peered at me closely, as the words rumbled out from his great chest. "You are saying that somebody could have passed me a cup at exactly the right moment to hand to Tyrestes? That would take such careful planning as to be almost impossible, I would think."

"Yes, sir, almost impossible. But to a determined individual, just *almost* impossible."

Nolarion looked away, his gaze sweeping the myriad of Ionian citizens milling about the outside of the hippodrome. His hand continued to stroke his long beard, but the action was more determined now, as if imbued with new purpose. I could barely hear his next words, he spoke them so softly.

"So it could have been some person other than a pouring girl or a magistrate," he mused. His eyes swung back to my face. "*Who*, Bias, who was it?"

"I am not sure yet, sir," I stammered, surprised by the ferocious expression on his big face. "It is simply another possibility that I must investigate further." He shook his massive head as if emerging from a pool of water, and the fierce countenance relaxed.

"Of course—pardon me," he murmured. Again, I had to strain to hear him. He shrugged, and smiled wanly. "Let us forget it for the moment, eh, young Bias? We will put it aside, and watch my son win the chariot race, eh?"

"As you say, magistrate," I agreed, bowing and moving away. Nolarion straightened up, squared his wide shoulders, and began making his way toward the owners' entrance.

The charioteers' and owners' area was a roped-off section of the grounds that emptied onto the hippodrome track through one of the gates in the wall. Inside the area red-faced aristocrats and rich merchants were bawling last minute instructions and warnings to harassed young drivers, who were obviously trying their best to seem respectful and attentive. Down on the track itself, I counted twenty-eight of the chariots in rows of six with four unlucky ones huddled miserably in the last row. All were of a similar design, being constructed of lightweight and springy wood, and were painted in all the colors of the rainbow. Bright reds, yellows, and oranges predominated, set off by white or black, but there were some shades of blue and green as well. The horses, being led up to the chariots by sweating, swearing trainers and slaves, were gaily caparisoned as well, with colored streamers affixed to their harnesses, manes, and tails.

Just inside the roped enclosure to my left I spotted the aristocrat Kreton speaking earnestly with a short, stocky driver, whose head was bobbing in apparent agreement every few seconds. Next to him outside the rope stood Krelonan the wrestler and two other gigantic young men. They were all laughing in a boisterous and carefree manner, each with a hamlike fist wrapped around a large kylix of wine. Obviously these were Kreton's prodigious trio of sons, and gods above, were they huge! Each one of them could easily have made two of me. Then, for just a moment, Krelonan stepped back, and revealed a dazzling girl in a fawn-colored chiton, staring fixedly into the throng within the enclosure. Her curling golden hair streamed down her back, festooned with a leafy vine, and her figure was perfect, high-breasted and small-waisted. Her creamy complexion seemed to be natural and twin areas of rosy color accentuated her high cheekbones. This must be the beautiful Bilassa, I conjectured approvingly, my breath caught in my throat. No wonder Tyrestes was interested in this one! My eyes were drawn away from her to the object of her unwavering gaze, but it seemed to be just a slim, boyish charioteer in a black tunic chatting quietly with his trainer off by themselves. Not recognizing him, I turned aside and bumped unceremoniously into Euphemius, the third magistrate with the iron-gray beard and stooped storklike posture.

"Your pardon, sir," I apologized with a short bow, as he straightened up and peered at me down his long hawks' beak of a nose. I saw him look at my cropped hair and black tunic, and nod in approval. Close behind him stood a handsome young man whom I supposed was his companion.

"Young Bias, eh?" Euphemius' tone was surprisingly high-pitched and reinforced the impression that he had been transformed from some long-legged marsh bird. "How goes your inquiry into the demise of the unfortunate Tyrestes?"

"It proceeds, sir, but not at a very good pace. The whole situation is so confusing and twisted. It's like being in a maze in the dark of night!" His birdlike black eyes twinkled at this description, and he nodded again.

"I think you will find that any inquiry into the minds and affairs of your fellow men will lead you to an identical conclusion. When the gods fashioned us after themselves, they included the infinite variety of thought and appearance that they themselves possess."

"Yes, sir, that is certainly true, but a little simplicity would not go astray here either. I have uncovered half a dozen people who may have had reason to do away with Tyrestes."

"Don't be so downhearted, Bias," he piped cheerfully. "There are probably another half dozen whom you have not uncovered!" This statement cheered me to no end, as you can imagine. I changed the subject.

"Magistrate, have you an entry in the race today?"

"Why, yes, I do," he admitted with a rueful snort, "but I do not expect to win now."

"Why is that, sir? Surely a man of your accomplishments and wisdom would supply the finest horses and the most able driver." It never hurts to be courteous to your elders, particularly when one is fishing for information. I noted Euphemius' young companion nodding in approval.

Euphemius flapped his skinny arms in sudden irritation, his snowy chiton billowing about him, conjuring up a vision of his rising into the air like a startled stork.

"Well, I would have had a very good chance of winning," he complained. "I have a magnificent set of runners, you see. They are the brown ones over there, hooked to that yellow and white chariot. But Tyrestes was to be my charioteer, you see, and with him dead, where was I to find another?" I suppose I must have gaped at this admission, for he bobbed his head several times and repeated this amazing revelation.

"Oh, yes, didn't you know? Tyrestes did not have enough wealth to supply his own team, but he was an excellent horseman. He and I agreed some six months ago that he would drive for me, since we would both obviously benefit from this arrangement. He would get another win to add to his overall glory, and I would gain the ultimate honor of having the winning team. He has been practicing racing at my estate ever since that time, attended to by his brother Usthius and my trainer, Lacramos."

"Who did you find to replace him at this late date?"

"Oh, the only one who could possibly replace him was his brother, you see? He was the only citizen who has worked with my horses, other than Tyrestes himself. Tyrestes let him drive the team several times during training to get the feel of them and whet his interest for the next set of games. I approve of that sort of interest in the young. So, when Tyrestes died, who else could I get but Usthius to drive at these games?"

"Usthius is driving your chariot?" I asked stupidly.

"Yes, of course," Euphemius replied impatiently. "Isn't that what I just said? There he is, over there, talking to my trainer, Lacramos."

He pointed a long, thin finger across the enclosure to the slim, boyish charioteer in black, who had been the object of Bilassa's intense interest.

CHAPTER XIII

THE CROWD ERUPTED INTO new heights of wild shouting and waving as the athletes entered the hippodrome through the gate in the wall.

Only the charioteers entered the track area itself. The owners either stayed in the roped enclosure or hurried back to their advantageous seats in the stands, some torn between the desire to be recognized as an entry owner and the need to obtain the best view of the race itself.

Arms raised high over their heads, the drivers rotated this way and that to the delight of the crowd, as they strode to their waiting chariots. This was one of few events not conducted in the nude at the Panionic Games, and each athlete sported a tunic in the colors of his patron. This was extremely unusual, in that Ionian men normally wore tunics of white or brown, so the effect heightened the feeling of novelty and excitement. The only exception I could see was Usthius dressed in black in mourning for his brother. I also noticed that his hair, while shorter than the fashion, had not been shorn as mine had. A fleeting thought, quick as the feet of Hermes the messenger god, raced through my mind that my mother need not have been quite so conscientious when she gave me a mourner's haircut.

I recognized several of the charioteers as they proceeded to their carts and climbed aboard, most still waving and grinning at the throng. Usthius walked all the way back to the fourth row to claim his chariot and was gazing in apparent bewilderment at his fellow contestants. In the second row in a crimson chariot Habiliates brandished his whip over his head to the delight of the hundreds of howling Miletians. Endemion stood in his orange and white car in a tunic of identical colors in the third row, gesturing to people he knew along the walls. There were three other contestants from Priene in the contest, but most of the racers were from mighty Miletus or from the great horse city of Colophon. Kreton's stocky little driver stood grim and resolute in a cart in the last row, his hands already wound tightly about his reins.

The increasingly restless horses were now being held in place by the slaves and trainers by main force. In the second and fourth rows, teams of horses reared and bucked, swinging their holders about like leaves clinging to a thrashing branch in a strong wind. When these chariot races lurched into action one or more of the desperate holders were usually trampled in the charioteers' mad rush to surge forward, but this merely served to whet the mob's appetite for more blood and excitement. The trick, of course, was for the holders to run straight back toward the rear of the chariot lines in the hope that they could pop out of the back end before the drivers began maneuvering their horses for better position.

The interior wall of the track surrounded the grassy oval in the middle of the hippodrome. This wall, in contrast to the chest-high exterior fence, was only waist high, and was designed to keep the chariots on the track. Its height also allowed paid rescuers and debris cleaners to sprint onto the racing floor to try to snatch up fallen charioteers and drag off smashed chariots before the remaining teams completed another circuit. Sometimes they were successful and sometimes not. I must admit I have seen several charioteers ground, along with their rescuers, under hoof and wheel if they did not get out of the way in time. Every twenty paces or so down both lengths of the hippodrome track, pairs of slaves waited for the event to commence, their apprehension at being designated as rescuers clearly evident in their anxious stance.

In the center of the grassy middle oval stood a small wooden tower, the height of two tall men. A ladder rested along one of its sides, and I now spied a man in a flapping chiton climbing to the top. He reached the summit, slowly stood up straight, and raised his hands to signal the crowd to quiet itself. This took several minutes, but eventually the watchers fell silent enough to satisfy him. All eyes were upon him as he raised a red scarf above his head letting it wave in the wind for a moment. All of the athletes were staring fixedly at the starter, their hands twined in their reins and their bodies straining back against the pull of their horses. Most of the holders, in contrast, were gazing unblinking at their drivers, waiting for a signal to release the horses and begin their mad sprint toward the rear.

The starter, an old man whose white beard flapped in the breeze in perfect harmony with the red rag, suddenly released his hold on the cloth. It fluttered for the merest heartbeat above his head, and then the noise of the crowd blasted forth like an explosion of sound from a volcano!

The chariots lurched forward, as if all propelled by a single hand of the giant Atlas, and the holders frantically sprinted in the opposite direction. A blue and white wagon in the third row canted to its right just as its horses bounded off, catching a pair of holders on its railing as they tried to speed past. The rest of the slaves and trainers popped out of the dust at the far end of the starting rows, leaving only those two lying in the dirt as the chariots careened toward the far end of the hippodrome. Four slaves bounded over the low interior wall, scooped up the fallen holders between them, and dragged them unceremoniously back into the safety of the grass enclosure.

This race was to be ten circuits of the hippodrome, giving the charioteers plenty of time and opportunity for their carts to be smashed to pieces and themselves flung under the hooves of madly galloping horses. Of all the events at the Panionic Games the chariot race was far and away the most dangerous. Granted one could get beaten up very thoroughly in the boxing ring or have bones snapped in the wrestling circle, but these injuries were seldom fatal. On the other hand, men could and did get killed with great regularity within the confines of the great hippodrome.

Having swerved around the far end of the circuit with no accidents as yet, the carts were now barreling back down the other side of the track. Frenzied drivers lashed their animals as they jockeyed recklessly for position, because early possession of the innermost position could mean the difference between a win and a loss. Second or third place in the great games did not exist—the only place that mattered was first. I saw the strained faces of Habiliates and Endemion flash by, their whip arms rising and falling as if signalling the gods for assistance.

The first accident occurred when the racers crowded up at my end of the hippodrome. Attempting to gain an interior position, a red and black entry from Ephesus made its move too soon and was instantly reduced to a bundle of flying sticks, when its near wheel caught on the projecting axle of a competitor from Clazomenae. The driver was catapulted into the path of a team of nervous horses from Miletus, who tried to shy away from the sudden object, only to collide with the next cart over. Both of those chariots immediately went down, the horses and drivers disappearing in a cloud of dust, chariots, and screaming animals. As the rest of the teams streamed past, the rescuers rushed out to secure the three athletes and drag off the destroyed wagons. One of the injured drivers was stumbling about on his own feet, but the other two lay still and silent.

A horse with an obviously broken leg was thrashing on the ground a short distance down the track, having pulled free of its comrades in harness, but none of the rescuers was brave enough to try and tackle that problem. The other freed horses either continued to run in the race with nobody to direct them, or bounced around the inside of the oval, scattering rescuer slaves to the four winds.

Two, three, four circuits completed! The number of competitors on the field shrank as more accidents took out the foolish or the rash. I saw an athlete from Erythrae flung at least ten paces into the air, when his chariot smashed headlong into a disabled cart. He came crashing down on top of a team of horses from Priene, causing them to leap the small fence and run down three rescuers inside the interior oval. Their Prienean driver was tossed to the ground inside the grassy area, and shakily rose to his feet to the thunderous cheers of the crowd. The noise was deafening, steadily rising like a stiffening gale buffeting a ship at sea. People were yelling themselves hoarse, some tearing at their clothes and hair as their favorites went down beneath the hooves of their rivals.

By the seventh circuit only sixteen chariots remained in the race. Destroyed carts, bits and pieces of wood, and dead and injured horses littered the track, making it appear that a battle had taken place there. The rescuers were able to snatch up all the drivers with only one of their number being run down on the track itself, but there had been too many accidents for them to be able to clear the racing arena of all the rapidly accumulating debris. At every stage of the race now, there seemed to be some object in the path of the careening chariots.

Instead of screaming with the many other viewers, I had gone deathly silent. I could not utter a word. It was as if my tongue had been torn away with the lives of the fallen drivers and horses, and I could only stare, transfixed, as the chariots continued to race around the hippodrome.

A massive pileup in the middle of the eighth circuit eliminated another six chariots, including that of Euphemius, which had been whipped along by the boyish Usthius. The first cart to swing around the near side of the curve collided with a deranged set of driverless horses galloping in the wrong direction, causing instant chaos as the following teams smashed into the pile one by one. I watched in horrified fascination as Usthius gallantly tried to swing his team out of the way to the right, only to have his leftmost horse nearly climb onto the chariot of the man in front. His chariot became hopelessly entangled, as he was flung off to the side. When the remaining teams had swept by and the rescuers ran onto the track, I noticed with mixed feelings that Usthius was stumbling toward the interior wall under his own power.

Habiliates of Miletus had hung on fiercely in the middle of the charging mass of racers the whole time, and now made his move in the ninth circuit. Whipping his horses as if he was pursued by the hounds of Artemis, he flew to the lead position while he rounded the near corner, closely pursued by Endemion and a competitor from Erythrae. What happened next was as unbelievable as it was dramatic. As Habiliates' chariot swerved violently around the corner, it rose up on the outside wheel, and then simply disintegrated, as the wheel snapped cleanly off at the hub. I had never seen anything like it. At one moment he was leading the field, and at the next his chariot was no longer there at all. I saw him hit the ground running, and it looked as if he had a chance to avoid the two teams bearing down on him from behind. As I have said before, I believe he was the fastest man I ever saw. But this last time he was not fast enough. Just as he was within leaping distance of the exterior wall, the rightmost horse of Endemion clipped him on the shoulder as it surged past. Knocked violently to the ground he had half risen to his knees, when the team from Erythrae dashed over him, crushing him to the ground, and then throwing his mangled body against the chest-high wall. The rescuers rushed to drag him out as the other competitors bounded past.

Endemion now held the lead and he kept it to the end, just holding off the Erythraean, whose team had been momentarily slowed by its encounter with the charioteer from Miletus. Our charioteer swept past the finish line one length ahead of his rival, his horses streaming blood from their many whip cuts, as they responded to his frantic urgings. Endemion and Priene had triumphed in the chariot race.

I turned back from the spectacle of hundreds of cheering onlookers pouring over the far wall onto the track and surrounding the victor and his exhausted team. Fighting my way through the crowd, I at last found myself staring down at Habiliates, as he lay broken and twisted at the edge of the stone fence. His bloody head lay in the lap of a distraught Ossadia, who was clasping him tightly and rocking back and forth, the red staining her white chiton as she wailed. The small magistrate Valato stood a few paces away, watching helplessly, his bewildered eyes begging me for assistance with his hysterical daughter.

It took a while for the crowds to melt away and head back to the city for further entertainment or back to their houses and campsites to begin preparing the evening dorpon meal. I initially helped Valato disentangle Ossadia from Habiliates. The magistrate could not understand why his daughter was so beside herself with grief over a Miletian athlete, and I was not about to be the one to tell him that I suspected it was because the two might be lovers. I kept remembering the scene from my dream. We finally succeeding in tearing her from the charioteer's body, and it was borne away by the servants of his rich patron, Polearchus of Miletus. Valato's wife Myrnia took charge at this point, and showing surprising strength of purpose, gathered up Ossadia in her arms, and crooned softly to her, until she quieted down enough to be led away herself. An emotionally exhausted Valato thanked me profusely for my assistance, and trailed off despondently after his wife and daughter, still apparently no wiser as to why the girl had temporarily lost her sanity.

I hung about the grounds for a time, congratulating Nolarion on his son's victory. The big aristocrat was all smiles and good feelings, and had bluff, kind words to say about everything. He was sorry for the untimely demise of Habiliates, but not overmuch, I thought. After all, he was well aware that this fortuitous death considerably improved his son's chances of becoming the games' champion. Endemion himself apparently simply chalked it up to being Apollo's favorite for the day. On some other day it might be his turn to be killed in the competition, but not today.

My family left for home while I was assisting Valato, for which I was quietly grateful. I did not much feel like participating in a drawn-out discussion of the intricacies of the race with my father, who tended to view competitions scientifically and would probably have dissected each point about each athlete's death with relish. My mother said she was glad the accidents had happened far enough away from the girls to shield them from the sight of bloodshed. Arlana, tightly grasping the hands of Tirah and Tapho as they climbed down the wobbling stands, commented loudly that she was convinced that the whole contest was merely a sop to the gods of men, as opposed to the sensible sacrifices demanded by goddesses. Risalla looked at me disdainfully and refused to answer when I asked her how she felt about Usthius being eliminated from the race.

As the last of the spectators were departing from the hippodrome, and the last of the horses and chariots being bundled away back to their stables, I was confronted by a dark-visaged slave. Appearing in front of me like a wraith and bowing low, he inquired if I was Bias of Priene. When I admitted that I was indeed the holder of this dubious honor, he politely asked me to follow him, as his master Polearchus desired to speak with me. Recognizing the name of Habiliates' patron, I acquiesced and padded behind him to an entourage at the far end of the hippodrome. As I approached, Polearchus rose to his feet, offered me a welcome kylix of wine, and motioned me to sit down. He was a short, compact man with a dark, spade-like beard, and reminded me more of a Lydian than an Ionian. He wasted no time, but proceeded directly to his point.

"You watched the race, of course?" he asked gently. His eyes were black and luminous, and stared directly into mine.

"Of course, noble Polearchus. Let me express my condolences over the death of your driver, Habiliates. He was a superb athlete, and I am sure he would have brought great glory to Miletus had he lived."

"He was more than my driver," stated the Miletian baldly. "He was my nephew, the only son of my only sister. I regarded him almost as a son, since I have no children myself. I believe he would have been the games champion had this not happened. I do not know how my sister will bear his death. He was all she lived for." He paused, and stared at the horizon, as he battled for composure. It took him a few moments.

"I hear you have been given a warrant by the city fathers of Priene to investigate the death of one of your own athletes, the noble Tyrestes," he continued, smiling sadly. "He was the competitor I was most afraid would beat Habiliates, you know. I admit I did not mourn overmuch when he died. But now I view things differently. I would like you to see something in your capacity as investigator." He spoke the last word as if it were a foreign term, and he did not approve of it very much.

We rose and walked over to the wreckage of a chariot, where a servant was waiting expectantly. The servant bowed low to both of us and stood waiting.

"This is Machus, my Carian carpenter and chariot maker." Polearchus gestured at the servant. "He is the best man with wood I have ever known. I think perhaps the nymphs of the trees are in love with him, he can accomplish so much with wood." The compact Miletian paused again, and then motioned for Machus to speak.

"Illustrious Bias of Priene, it was I who constructed the chariot that raced today with the team of Polearchus. It is undoubtedly the best work I have ever done. I shall never make one so fine again, now that we are burdened with the shade of Habiliates crying out for justice."

"What do you mean?" I asked curiously. "Why should Habiliates' shade cry out for justice?"

"Observe, noble Bias," Machus said, and led me to the wheel of the destroyed chariot. Bending down, he touched the axle lightly and traced his finger around the area where it had broken away.

"Do you see how even and smooth this break is?"

"Why, yes," I replied, bending down and running my own fingers over the break. "It is amazing that it broke off so cleanly, eh?"

"It is not amazing at all," the carpenter contradicted flatly. "The wheel did not just break off. The axle was sawed nearly through and dabbed with paint to hide the marks. It was simply a matter of time during the stress of the race that it would break off, and this is what happened. Since the most stress to this wheel would occur when it rounded a corner of the track, that is the most likely place the *accident* would occur. It did precisely that."

"You mean that somebody tampered with this chariot wheel? How would they know when it would break?" I tried to mask my incredulity.

"They would not have to know," replied Machus. "It was enough that it should break any time during the race. Habiliates' injury or death was not necessary. The only thing that was necessary was that the wheel should break."

"So you see why I asked you over here," interrupted Polearchus harshly, staring at me with reddened, angry eyes. "My nephew did not just die in an accident of the games. In effect, he was murdered, just as surely as your Tyrestes was murdered."

CHAPTER XIV

"Good evening, noble Polearchus." Valato spoke as warmly as he could under the circumstances, leading the Miletian by the arm through the prodomus and left into the andron room. In the background we could hear a steady keening, like the whistling of the wind through a narrow tunnel or the plaintive cry of some seabird.

"My daughter, " explained the small magistrate apologetically, gesturing toward the rear of his house. "She is in mourning for your nephew, Habiliates, although I can't understand why she is so affected by his shade's passing. She didn't even know him. I can only assume it is her sensitive nature that causes her to bewail the end of such a fine young man."

He shook his bald head and smiled sadly.

Polearchus and I shot each other a knowing look, and then returned our attention to our host. I had explained many of my suspicions to the short dark aristocrat from the giant city across the bay, and he confessed that he knew that his nephew had been secretly seeing some female. Until now he had not known who she was.

We were gathered at the estate of Valato on the evening of the chariot race. I had sent messages by courier to the three magistrates, telling them that I and Habiliates' uncle desired to speak with them. Valato had informed all concerned that he was constrained to stay at home that night because of his daughter's indisposition, and kindly requested all of us to meet at his house. It was still light when we arrived: days were growing longer as summer approached, and we had no need of oil lamps to help us find his mansion.

And mansion it was. It was built like a typical Ionian farm estate from native stone and mud brick, but it was twice as large as my father's modest house.

Two squat towers guarded the entrance to the prodomus, lending it the appearance of a miniature fortress, and a landscaped path bordered by flowers and shrubs wound its way up the small hill to the front door. Valato's wealth lay in his olive groves, and the orderly ranks of gnarled trees marched away in all directions from his palace like obedient soldiers guarding a stronghold.

The andron to which we were led was already occupied by Nolarion, Euphemius, and to my surprise, Crystheus. I certainly had not informed the major priest of my intended meeting, but Nolarion imperiously admitted that he thought it would be a good idea for Poseidon's representative to be present.

The magistrates all greeted the Miletian courteously and reclined on klines. Polearchus said that he would prefer a chair, giving some indication that this might not be a friendly visit, and the Prienians glanced at each other significantly. I also sat in a chair next to the visitor to lend him my support, for what good it might do, and the servants brought another chair for Crystheus.

It turned out that Polearchus needed nobody's support to tell his tale, particularly not my poor offering. Just as he had done with me earlier in the day, the Miletian went directly to the point without any flowery preliminaries.

"I have spoken at some length with your investigator, the illustrious Bias," he began darkly, letting his eyes flicker back and forth among the three city officials. "He and I have determined that my nephew, Habiliates, was murdered this afternoon during the chariot race." He and I?

You could have heard a chiton pin drop in that room. Valato stared in consternation. Euphemius's eyes darted between Polearchus and me, his hands plucking at his snowy garment. The muscular Nolarion's gaze narrowed and his mouth curled down slightly at the corners. Crystheus, in his corner, broke the silence by a disbelieving cough.

"Surely this is not the case," he protested pompously. "It must have been an accident, an unfortunate accident to be sure, but still an accident." His hands were outspread in front of him as if he were warding off some malevolent spell thrown out by the dark foreigner. Polearchus speared him with a contemptuous look, and the priest shrank back into his chair.

"It was *murder*!" Polearchus barked. "We and the chariot's maker examined the chariot and could plainly see that the axle had been sawn through and disguised with paint. It was deliberate cold-blooded murder accomplished by some whoreson who wanted to make sure my nephew did not win that race!"

Nolarion was the first magistrate to respond.

"Bias?" he asked softly, his narrowed eyes settling on me. "You examined this chariot and came to the same conclusion?" I could feel Polearchus stiffen beside me, realizing that the big magistrate had in effect doubted his word.

"Yes, sir!" I stated strongly, dispelling any possible doubt any of them might have. "Our *guest* and I are completely in agreement. The chariot had been tampered with, just as he says."

"But tampering with a chariot does not mean that murder was intended." Nolarion's large hands stroked his luxuriant black beard. "Perhaps the object was an accident to take Habiliates out of the race, rather than kill him?"

"What does it matter what the object was?" interrupted Polearchus harshly. "My kinsman is dead. I demand retribution!" He raised his fists above his head and shook them. The magistrates stared back at him sympathetically but in some confusion.

"My dear sir, we certainly agree with you that retribution by your family is warranted, if this is a case of murder," agreed Valato quickly. "But how do we find the culprit?"

"And, really, what does it have to do with us?" asked Euphemius querulously. "We can't identify every madman who attends the Panionic Games. Why, there are thousands of people here from all over Ionia!"

The Miletian stared around the room in dumbfounded anger, as if he could not believe his ears. I rose quickly from my chair to forestall an outbreak from him.

"Gentlemen," I began quietly but firmly, "I do not believe you fully understand the implications here. I think that the deaths of Tyrestes and Habiliates may be related. The crimes may even have been committed by the same person." I paused for effect, and went on, "In that case, this is not simply a case of murder, foul though that may be. There could now be a guestslayer among us!"

The word "guestslayer" reverberated through the andron like a thunderclap. Nolarion bared his teeth like a wolf and half rose from his kline. Euphemius again played the stork, flapping his arms distractedly, his eyes boring into mine. I could hear the hiss of Valato's indrawn breath and saw him grab at a kylix of wine for a few precious gulps.

You see, as bad as murder was, guestslaying was infinitely worse. To an Ionian the hospitality of his city and the pride that he took in its accomplishments was all-important. Guestslaying meant that an invited person, who trusted in that hospitality, had been betrayed to die an ignominious death. While a murder infused the murderer, the victim's family, and his close friends with a deadly miasma, guestslaying clearly contaminated the entire city-state. A known guestslaying without appropriate retribution would reflect on the honor of every citizen of Priene, and even affect our relationship with Poseidon, our home deity.

"Why do you think this is a guestslaying?" Valato asked nervously, after he had swallowed his wine. The state of his agitation could be measured by the fact that he did not offer anybody else a kylix. I gathered my thoughts for a moment, reluctant to reveal too much about my conjectures.

"I don't say for certain that it is. But the similarities between the two deaths are interesting. First, murders are rare, as we all know, and here are two committed in the same city only a few days apart. Secondly, both victims are well-known athletes of great ability. Thirdly, they were both here in the city to participate in the great games. And lastly, several people whom I have connected to both young men were present at both murder sites."

"But this does not mean that Habiliates' murder was a guestslaying," complained Crystheus from his corner. "A citizen of Miletus or any city could have killed him."

"That's true," I admitted; the magistrates were nodding, obviously hoping that this was indeed the case. "But unless all these similarities are coincidences, then it *was* a guestslaying, because we *know* that Tyrestes was killed by a Prienian. Only citizens from our city were pouring wine or handling cups or jugs at the ceremony."

This clearly shook my listeners. Nolarion heaved a great sigh, then asked softly. "And who knows about the possibility that this was a guestslaying?"

Polearchus eyed him haughtily. "Only Bias, myself, and my carpenter know that Habiliates was murdered. That is, only we know it at this time."

"What do you mean by that, sir?" asked Valato, his deep voice booming out incongruously from his small chest.

"I shall tell you precisely what I mean," the Miletian spat back at him. "I mean this! I have said that my family demands retribution for this foul deed. You must find out who committed this crime and present him to me for justice in Miletus!"

"And if we cannot or do not find out?" asked Nolarion, almost whispering.

"Then I will announce this guestslaying to the multitudes gathered here," said Polearchus. "We will see how your city fares when I tell the crowd about Priene's evil heart on the last day of the games!"

"Do you mean to say that you are threatening us?" asked Crystheus in disbelief.

"Indeed I am, priest. You have three days to find the murderer. On the third day, the day of the pentathlon, I will ensure that every Ionian at these games knows about this unsolved guestslaying."

You must understand that this was indeed a potent threat. This was such a serious matter in most people's minds that it could affect the trade Priene conducted with her fellow cities, and almost certainly free travel to and from Priene. Miletus would surely be grievously insulted, a major blow to the most powerful of all Ionian city-states. What her reaction might be nobody could say. And the crowd itself? Would it react violently when informed that it had been sleeping, eating, and celebrating for the last three days in a town blanketed by the wicked miasma of guestslaying? I did not know, but I do know that I did not wish to find out.

Nor, apparently, did the city magistrates. They immediately tried to reassure the angry Polearchus.

"I can tell you, sir, that you do not need to make such a threat," cried Euphemius. "We shall get to the bottom of this matter, we shall indeed!"

"Yes, of course we shall," repeated Valato, his short brown beard bobbing with earnestness. "You know that the noble Bias is investigating the matter. He has already proved to us by his comments tonight that he is clearly giving it much thought and attention. Surely, he will find the culprit or culprits within the next day or two, eh Bias?"

He looked anxiously at me for confirmation.

"Of course, sir," I replied, bowing my head toward him.

"As a matter of fact, didn't you just say that you had connected several people to both athletes, and they were present at both murder sites?" asked Nolarion, so softly that I had to strain to hear him. "Tell us who they are and if you suspect them of any complicity in this matter, noble Bias."

As he spoke, the enormity of my mistake burst blindingly upon me. Yes, I had said precisely that, and his son was one of those people! As was the daughter of a major aristocrat of the city and the *noble* younger brother of one of the slain athletes. Gods above, I had not even ruled out the magistrates themselves yet, because of the possible dalliances of Valato's plain but fiery Ossadia and Nolarion's desire to see his son a champion!

"Those were just conjectures, gentlemen," I stammered. "I only listed them so that you would perceive the seriousness of the situation."

"Well, you certainly accomplished your objective," said the big magistrate dryly. "But conjecture or not, tell us who these people are that you suspect of these dreadful crimes?" All eyes looked expectantly at me, and I swallowed hard.

"No sir, I would rather not," I whispered weakly.

"What did you say?" asked Crystheus in astonishment. The magistrates were staring at me incredulously, as if I had just turned into Pan, complete with horns and hairy goat legs.

"I don't think that would be wise," I repeated, more strongly this time. "You have shown great confidence in my abilities by awarding me the honor of investigating this matter and finding the murderer. But I have discovered that I must have independence and secrecy if I am to accomplish this task."

"And you have discovered these needs in only a few days?" asked Nolarion, his sarcastic tone very evident. "Are we then to believe that this is all you have discovered? Is that why you don't wish to tell us whom you suspect?" Thank you, Poseidon, for showing me the way out!

"Indeed, that is not true, magistrate," I replied as stiffly as I could. "I have seen many people at both locations. Why, even Crystheus himself has been at both sites!" The mouth of the major priest fell open, as he stared at me and then at the bemused onlookers.

"Are you saying that the illustrious Crystheus is a suspect?" asked Euphemius wryly. "I propose that it would have been difficult for him to poison Tyrestes with one hand and kill the sacred bullock with the other!" Some strained laughter followed this remark, but at least the mood was broken.

"Of course, you are correct, sir," I agreed. "But you see, I have not spoken to all the suspicious parties, and I feel that to burden you at this time with my incomplete speculation would be tiring." It was clear that the whole conversation was becoming tedious to them by now, for which I thanked the god of the sea again.

"Oh, very well," said Valato, waving his hand in a gesture of dismissal. "Keep your secrets to yourself, Bias. But remember this—we expect you to find the answer to this puzzle if you wish to keep your good name and honor intact. We have no desire to see the noble Polearchus accuse the city of harboring a guestslayer, be it true or not."

He grimaced at the Miletian, reminding me of a bantam rooster displeased with some intruder in the farmyard. Polearchus scowled back at him, clearly not intimidated by him.

"I have great confidence in the ability of Bias to come to the bottom of this barrel of rotten fish," the Miletian snarled. "But his or anybody else's honor notwithstanding, I will keep my word about announcing it on the last day of the games. Now if you will excuse me, I must prepare my mourning garments for tomorrow."

As he rose from his chair, a new outburst of wild wailing came from the back of the house. Valato glanced quickly about, and smiled sadly again in apology.

CHAPTER XV

THREE DAYS! THE PENTATHLON, the crowning event of the games, would occur in just three days. And on that same day Polearchus would announce to the world that the city of Priene had been steeped in the dishonor of guestslaying for the entire period. Unless I found the murderer and revealed his or her identity to the powerful Miletian.

Why me? I thought morosely, as I trudged back to my father's farm under darkening skies. Why not get somebody else more suitable to investigate these foul murders? Of course, I knew the answer even as I asked the question. Crimes like this were so rare that there was no mechanism set up to investigate them. That was simply part of a magistrate's many duties, and the accused parties were turned over to the victim's family, whose job it was to convince the citizenry of their guilt.

I longed to see the murderer standing forlornly at the Podium of Justice in front of a large jury of citizens and confronted by his accusers from their Podium of Retribution.

But when I tried to visualize the face and form of the accused standing behind the stone block of the damned, the picture kept shifting in my mind. Who was the guestslayer?

The accused changed from Endemion to Nolarion to Valato to Ossadia to Bilassa to Usthius in a flashing display of my own incompetence. Gods above, even my own sister Risalla had been dallying with one of the suspects! What in Hades was I to do next?

As I reached the prodomus of our farm and entered the front door, I realized that I could only keep talking to people who may have been involved in the crimes and hoping that some minute piece of unguarded information would lead me to the answer. It occurred to me that I had not yet spoken to either Bilassa the daughter of Kreton or to Usthius the brother of Tyrestes. So the next order of business obviously had to be talking with them.

The household had again already finished the dorpon evening meal, but my mother had kept a plate of food for me on the table in the back garden. I lifted the cloth cover to discover a fine offering of maza bread, two boiled hen's eggs, and a mound of walnuts, small onions, and olives nestled in cabbage leaves. Next to it stood a small jug of wine and one of the family's old chipped kylixes. Much cheered by this motherly show of affection, I ate slowly by the light of a single olive oil lamp I had brought out from the house hallway.

"And has the young master discovered the identity of our nefarious murderer?" a quietly mocking (it seemed to me mocking, at any rate) voice inquired at my elbow. I started and turned to see Duryattes hovering close behind me, a slight smile on his face.

"Don't smirk," I ordered him, stuffing several olives and a cabbage leaf into my mouth. "Show a little proper respect, and quit sneaking up on me! And sit down, for Poseidon's sake." He plopped down on the bench next me, and eyed me carefully for a moment.

"My apologies, master," he said at length. "In truth I didn't mean to be disrespectful. Though might I venture a guess that our murderer's identity is still unknown at this point?"

"You venture correctly." I drank some wine, pushed my plate to one side, and looked at him thoughtfully. He had been quite adept at ferreting information for me in the agora and clearly had a quick, if somewhat rebellious, mind. Perhaps that young mind could discern pieces of the puzzle where mine could not? I was willing to admit that I could use any help I could get, but balked at bringing this youthful independent-minded servant into my full confidence. After all, he was not even Ionian! How much assistance could he really offer? Any help at all, I thought ruefully, is more than I have right now.

"Listen carefully, Duryattes," I cautioned him, staring straight into those intelligent, amused eyes. "I'll tell you all that has happened, and you will not speak until I have finished. Then you will tell me what you think happened and who is responsible." At these words the amusement visibly fled from him like a shade fleeing from a dying body, and he nodded gravely, giving me his full attention.

His eyes widened as I told him about my conversation with Risalla about her meeting with Usthius and Usthius' new position as head of his family. I described my talks with the various spectators at the chariot race, the death of Habiliates, the intervention of his uncle Polearchus, and the misgivings of the magistrates at our recent meeting at Valato's house. I mentioned the strange reaction of Ossadia to the charioteer's death and Valato's seeming bewilderment at the reason for her mourning.

The boy did not say a word for several minutes after I finished, but stared thoughtfully at the orb of the moon, his face illuminated by the light of the goddess Selene, as she began to drive her shining steeds across the night sky. When he did speak, he was deadly serious.

"It is clear, young master, that we need more information if we are to apprehend this evil person." I noted wryly that he used the word *we*. However, I had made my decision and was pleased that he had accepted the challenge.

"Let's analyze each person that you suspect, and decide what further information we need to confirm or deny that person's guilt or innocence," Duryattes continued. "First, we have Endemion the athlete, and closely connected to him is his father Nolarion. You have spoken to them both, in fact several times to the magistrate. Endemion knows that Tyrestes is more popular than he, and even though he does not wish to admit it, that Tyrestes is probably a more skilled athlete. If Endemion is to win any glory for himself and Priene, it would be very helpful if Tyrestes did not compete. But Tyrestes is young, strong, and an intense competitor, so it would appear that there is only one sure way to eliminate him from the games. His father Nolarion must feel the same way. Didn't you say that he was once the champion of Priene?"

I nodded. "Yes, he won the pentathlon and several other events in the games twenty years ago. He's probably the best athlete the city has ever produced."

"Well, then, there is his reason for the killing. He could have decided to relive his glory through the exploits of his son. When he realized that Tyrestes was the better athlete, his dreams would demand the elimination of that threat. And note, young master, that both men had the opportunity to kill him. The father handed the cup to the unfortunate Tyrestes, and the son was next to him the whole time. It would have been simple for either of them to tamper with the cup or its contents.

"In fact," the slave added brightly, "they could have planned and executed the crime together to ensure Endemion's chances of winning the laurel crown!"

I must admit that this possibility had not occurred to me. My idea of including Duryattes in my considerations was already bearing fruit.

"But what about Habiliates the Miletian athlete?" I asked. "What are your ideas on his murder by one or both of these men?"

Duryattes licked his lips and reconsidered the glories of Selene. "Well, the motive would be the same, wouldn't it? Habiliates was extremely fast and was the favorite to win most, if not all, of the running events. I understand he was also very skilled at jumping and throwing the javelin, which would have made him also the favorite in the pentathlon, despite his indifference to the wrestling event. Eliminate him, and suddenly Endemion is at the top of the heap, as far as the competitions go. He is a very well-rounded athlete, and may now be able to win enough events to bring the crown back to Priene and his father's house!"

"But what about the opportunity to eliminate Habiliates? Machus the carpenter showed me where the chariot's axle had been sawed nearly through. Wouldn't it take a long time to do that, and how could you know when the axle would break?"

The boy glanced at me with just a trace of disdain.

"Young master," he said patiently. "Have you ever sawed through a sapling with a small sharp bronze saw?" I shook my head.

"It would be quick work," he explained. "Then dab on a bit of grease or paint and nobody could tell the difference. It could have been done that very morning, since all the chariots are kept in the games stables by the hippodrome, aren't they? Yes, it would have been child's play. Who cares *when* the accident occurs, as long as it *does* occur? The chances of a charioteer being injured in such an accident are probably quite high."

"And the reason the axle did not break until late in the race was because Habiliates was a careful driver, and did not put undue pressure on the sawed joint until he made his dash for the lead," I concluded for the boy. He nodded smugly. We were both silent for a while, considering these possibilities.

"Let us proceed to the female side of the equation," I suggested. "What do you think about that?"

"Young master, it seems that our own Tyrestes was a sexual athlete as well as an athlete in the normal sense of the word. It also seems that he was searching for a way to rescue his family's fortunes by finding a wife who would arrive with a large dowry. You agree?" I nodded my head reluctantly, not wishing to think ill of the dead, but forced by honesty to agree with him.

"It is possible he dallied with both these young girls," Duryattes said, holding up two fingers. He ticked off his points with his other hand. "We have word through the gossip at the agora that he may have bedded Bilassa, the daughter of the rich aristocrat Kreton. We also know that he at least talked several times with Ossadia the daughter of the magistrate Valato. Might he have done more than talked?"

I thought back to my conversation with Ossadia in the tunnel entrance to the stadium, where her repressed passion had permeated the air. I shook my head tentatively.

"I don't think so." I scratched the top of my shorn pate. "She seemed much more interested in Habiliates, and her behavior after his death would seem to confirm her devotion to the Miletian."

"On the other hand, does her interest in Habiliates eliminate the possibility that she slept with Tyrestes?" Duryattes asked. I considered this possibility.

"No, I suppose it doesn't eliminate it. Ossadia struck me as the kind of woman who would bed whomever she pleased whenever she pleased."

"Then it's equally possible that she compared the two lovers, Tyrestes and Habiliates, and decided to kill Tyrestes in order to—one, keep him from telling anybody about her dalliances and thus ruining her future, or two, destroy an impediment to Habiliates winning the games," the slave concluded triumphantly. I thought this a little far-fetched, but possible.

"And what about Bilassa's motives?" I asked. Duryattes waved his hand negligently in the air.

"That one is even easier! After being bedded by our hero, she learns that he is speaking to Ossadia and her father about a possible match. She's furious, but she bides her time until the right moment and then coldly poisons him. Remember, she too has a lot to lose if her family or some suitor learns about her adventures."

"And Habiliates? What motive would either of the women have for killing him and how could they do it?" The boy's brow furrowed as he seemed to contemplate the olive trees in the moonlight.

"I must admit I can't see a reason for Ossadia to murder Habiliates," he said, "but I think Bilassa had an excellent reason. Besides avenging herself on Tyrestes, she could also punish Ossadia by killing her lover. As for the how, all large estates have carpenter slaves who could innocently, or not so innocently, give advice on how to disable a chariot. In fact, in many cases the slave could be persuaded to assist his mistress to pursue her honor by doing the deed himself." He shrugged his narrow shoulders.

"I can think of a reason for Ossadia killing Habiliates," I interjected. "If she too had been bedded by the Miletian and was then rejected, that would be plenty of reason." I recalled her smoldering desire during our conversation and shivered. Again the two of us were silent as we let our minds ramble in the gaze of the moon goddess. The air was growing chilly now, and I rubbed my upper arms, noting with distaste the black streaks of dye on them.

"And so, young master, that brings us to Usthius, the younger brother of Tyrestes," said Duryattes, his skinny arms wrapped around himself. "He had both reason and opportunity to do away with his brother, eh? If Tyrestes dies,

Usthius inherits the estate, poor though it may be, and can negotiate for his choice of wife when he wishes to. Do we know anything about the relationship between these two brothers?" I shook my head again.

"No, I haven't yet been able to speak with Usthius. My family didn't know them well. Risalla has spoken twice to Usthius in the agora and again at the wine pouring ceremony, but she didn't say anything about the men's feelings or rivalries. But she did say that Tyrestes had squelched Usthius' hopes of mating with her. She thought it was funny!"

I paused and then continued, "And what of the death of Habiliates? How could Usthius be mixed up in that?" I rose from the cool bench and began to pace back and forth. Duryattes watched me for a moment, before he spoke.

"You mentioned to me that you thought Bilassa seemed very interested in Usthius at the chariot race? Where he was driving the team of Euphemius in place of Tyrestes?"

I nodded at him once more; his eyes gleamed as he too rose to his feet and walked excitedly about.

"Consider this, young master! Isn't it possible that Bilassa either killed Tyrestes by herself or with Usthius? If she wanted to be mistress of her own estate, either brother would do. She could have murdered the elder brother because he was no longer interested in her and then turned her attention to the younger brother. Or they could have plotted together to do away with Tyrestes so that they could wed!"

"That's a possible scenario," I admitted. "But let's return to Habiliates. What possible reason could Usthius have for killing him?"

"There is a double reason for Usthius to have murdered his older brother, you know. Not only did killing Tyrestes gain him an estate. It also gained him entrance to participation in the games without having to endure years of training and discipline. The chariot race is the most chancy of all the events—anybody can win in that race depending on sheer bad luck on everybody else's part! That could also give him a reason for eliminating Habiliates, an excellent charioteer. Even without Bilassa urging Usthius on, the younger brother would greatly increase his chances of winning by a little judicious sawing. He could even have tampered with other chariots. We only know about Habiliates' chariot, because his was the only one that crashed on its own!"

Even as I contemplated these assertions, considering that they bordered on absurdity, the niggling thought came to me that people did very strange things out of envy, hatred, or greed. While it seemed ridiculous to think that Usthius would sabotage Habiliates' chariot to eliminate a racing rival, it seemed chillingly possible that he might do it at the behest of the vengeful Bilassa. Her beauty could spur a man to commit many crimes, I thought.

"Young master, there is one more possibility you must consider." Duryattes stood as still as a statue. What happened to the *we* of such a short time before, I wondered.

I received my answer in his next sentence.

"By her own admission your sister Risalla has been involved with Usthius. We don't know how deep this involvement runs—as we have only her word that it was a few conversations in the marketplace. Although Usthius could have murdered Tyrestes because he refused to consider Risalla as Usthius' bride, it is equally possible that your sister could have helped him. As the wife of Usthius, she would be the mistress of her own estate before her two elder sisters."

I had listened to this quiet argument with growing anger and disbelief. How dare this boy accuse a lady of his own household of such a deed. Hadn't he been raised with Risalla, playing together around the grounds for years? My face must have reflected my growing anger, because he looked at me and stepped back.

My pent-up frustration burst out suddenly, and I reached for him with a snarl! Much more nimble than I, he scampered around the edge of the table, and I banged my shin soundly against the bench in front of me. The searing pain burned the anger out of me as I hopped about swearing and sank back down on the bench vigorously rubbing my injured limb. Duryattes eyed me warily from the other side of the table, ready to jump either way at an instant's notice.

"Come and sit down, boy," I said wearily. "You have my apologies. I wasn't angry with you, but rather at the whole situation. Of course, we must consider the possibility of Risalla's involvement. Of course we must."

Duryattes carefully skirted the table and eased himself down on the opposite end of my bench. He broke into a quick grin when he saw that my apology was genuine.

"I'm sorry I had to bring it up, young master. I agree it is not very likely, but does one ever get to really know other people? I mean, really get to know their thoughts and desires, and what they are truly capable of doing?" I stared at him in astonishment, as he nodded like some old sage.

"At any rate, our next move seems quite clear," he went on. Ah, the *our* was back again. "You must speak separately to both Bilassa and Usthius, and note their reactions to your many questions!"

"I had already reasoned that out, my dear Duryattes," I said dryly. "But how am I to go about it? Bilassa is guarded by her Atlas-like brothers, and Usthius certainly has no reason to cooperate with me."

"Just as you have reasoned that this must be done, young master, I have reasoned out *how* it will be done," he asserted, his eyes twinkling in the night. "You will recall that I am acquainted with Bilassa's maid, the one who spoke up in the marketplace about her mistress's indiscretions. When we attend the competitions tomorrow, I will seek her out and convince her to arrange for her mistress to meet with you."

I was filled with admiration. This boy was crafty enough to go far!

"And in the case of Usthius," he added, "what could be simpler? I will deliver a message to him that you have learned of his improper interest in your sister Risalla and want to speak to him about the affair."

My admiration doubled.

"By the cunning of Pan, I think both those solutions may work!" I grinned at the boy across the bench. A look of alarm flooded his face.

"Young master, don't mention Pan when we are under the gaze of the moon goddess Selene," he whispered furiously. "Remember, he seduced her by turning himself into a snow-white ram in the forest!"

CHAPTER XVI

THE NEXT MORNING WAS one of those rare days in early summer with scudding gray clouds and light drizzling rain. The rainy season in Ionia generally runs from the month of Poseidon at the beginning of winter to the month of Elaphebolion at the beginning of spring. After that, Helios' chariot of the sun infrequently permits the raindrops to come between itself and Demeter's Earth. We farmers welcome a wet period now and then, since it helps the crops and allows us to get caught up on indoor chores.

Not on this misty day however. It was the fourth day of the great Panionic Games, and they would proceed come what may. I had sent out Duryattes immediately after our light ariston breakfast meal to locate Bilassa's maid and set the wheels in motion. A little later on, as my family ambled down the road toward the city, I went over the scheduled events of the day in my mind's eye. In the morning the excitement would begin with the initial rounds of the pancration fighting and the long jump and end with the long race, the twenty-four-stade distance running from the stadium to a turn-around point beyond the city limits and back to the stadium. I especially hoped to be able to view the long race, as I myself am not half bad at it, compared with all the other events, at which I am atrocious. Oh, yes, I can hurl a pretty fair javelin too, by the way. By measure of a clepsydra water clock, normally used for timing speeches in the meetings of the city Assembly, I can complete the long race in about one sixth of an hour, but of course, the athletes in the games would turn in times as good as a seventh of an hour. The long race was run only once during the games, and only first place counted for any glory. I suppose that must give some indication of the importance we Ionians, and indeed all the Greeks, give to winning, since second or third place is not even recognized in the events.

Of course, most of the spectators would be eager to watch the pancration, the bloody event that combined wrestling, boxing, and the game of dirty tricks. Its matches would continue upright or on the ground, until one of the contestants surrendered. Basically anything was allowed with the exception of eye gouging and biting, although only the gods knew why these were not permitted, since one could punch, kick, or strangle at will. It was a relatively new event, this being only the fourth Panionic Games that it appeared in, and according to my father, was a clear indication of the decline of our civilization. I must admit the contestants possessed prodigious strength and incredible endurance, but very little actual skill in athletics. Most of the competitors in the boxing and wrestling events stayed away from the pancration for fear they would be injured and unable to compete in events requiring more skill. Of course there were always athletes like Krelonan, the son of Kreton and brother of Bilassa, who believed they were invincible and could win in both the pancration and wrestling or boxing.

In the afternoon the crowd would be back at the hippodrome for the horse races.

Like the chariot races of the day before, the horse races tended to reflect more glory on the horse's owner than on its rider. But the rider did get his share of glory by receiving a crown as well. One had to be both extremely proficient and fortunate to win the horse race, as nearly everything was permitted there too. Riding bareback, neck and neck, the contestants could swerve their horses into their opponents' and even strike at the other riders alongside them. I hoped to be able to speak to Usthius at the hippodrome; Euphemius had told me last night that the young man would be riding for him, just as he had already employed him as chariot driver in place of the dead Tyrestes.

Finally, to end the day's events, the initial rounds of the discus throwing would take place at the stadium in the mid-afternoon after the horse racing. This third day of actual competition would complete the preliminary rounds of all the events, paving the way for the final rounds of the single events on the fourth day and the pentathlon on the fifth day. The games and festival would conclude with sacrifices and celebration in the afternoon and during the evening of the last day. That is, of course, if I was able to catch the murderer by then. If I failed in my task, Polearchus would reveal to the crowd, now at least 10,000 strong, that they had been enjoying themselves for the last two days in a city shrouded in the miasma of guestslaying. What would happen then, I did not care to imagine.

The people walking along the muddy road with us increased in number until we were in the midst of a large and boisterous crowd as we entered the city's western gate. It was not really a gate, just a point at which the road passed the city's outermost buildings, but it did have a tall pillar on each side where the normally hard-packed dirt of the country road changed to the closely fitted cobbles of the town. I have visited Miletus across the bay several times with my father, and that great metropolis had actual gates that opened and shut at various times, permitting or preventing entry to the city at the gatekeeper's whim. Amazing!

At any rate, my mother stopped the family at the western gate and drew us off to one side, my father fidgeting and clearly anxious to get to the stadium, although the long race, that he said he did not want to miss, did not take place for several hours, the early morning period being reserved for the pancration, which he professed to disdain. My mother had no intention of letting her younger daughters view the pancration.

"My love, I don't want to miss any of the long race," protested Holicius to Tesessa, as she fussed with the set of his cloak on his shoulders and the curls of his beard. She produced a tiny set of bronze scissors from a fold in her own chiton, and gave his beard a judicious snip or two, as he stood suffering silently.

"My dear, you are undoubtedly the most noble-looking man I have seen on the road today," she said cheerfully. "I am sure people will notice your entry into the stadium, whenever you arrive!"

Holicius preened like a small bird fluffing his plumage, and smiled affectionately at his wife.

"Bias and I will take the girls with us to the stadium and not let them out of our sight," he said. "You go and view a comedy, eh?"

My mother had unbent enough to allow Ulania, Arlana, and after a tearful session of pleading, Risalla, to attend the morning events with my father and me. She would not listen to Tirah's equally histrionic pleas to attend the games.

"Thank you, husband," Tesessa murmured. "We will meet you in time for mid-day deipnon meal at the hippodrome, then?" Holicius impatiently nodded and hurried off, followed by the three girls like chicks trailing a bantam rooster. I gave my mother a quick smile and brought up the rear of the procession, as a good guard should do. Our male slave Dryses flashed me a wry grin as I passed him, and plodded along after my mother, being the designated protector that day for the younger girls.

Duryattes was anxiously awaiting our arrival as we reached the stadium gate, springing up and down in an effort to see over the heads of taller people in his way.

He spotted our party as we came within easy view, and worked his way through the entering throng toward us, like a snake slithering over a field strewn with rocks.

I motioned for him to follow us to our prearranged seats near the stadium floor. It took us at least one half hour to get to the seats, as my father stopped to greet each aristocratic citizen he met on the way and chat for a few moments about the games or the weather. By the time Holicius and the girls were seated, Duryattes was squirming like an eel with his pent-up news.

"Young master, I have met and spoken with Bilassa's maid," he whispered, as we watched the athletes on the stadium floor preparing to batter one another into submission.

"Well?" I asked, pretending indifference as I viewed the preparations on the field.

"Well, she has carried a message to her mistress that you wished to talk with her alone, and the time is now, now!" I stole a glance at my father. He was conversing animatedly with a friend to his left, but Arlana was contemplating me with a fishy eye. Ulania was peering about shortsightedly—for her betrothed, no doubt, and Risalla was gazing hungrily at the contestants stretching and flexing in the area below. I bestowed a sweet smile on Arlana, who turned away abruptly to engage Ulania in conversation.

"Follow me," I mouthed to Duryattes, who slid along in my wake as I made my way back to the stadium entrance.

"For Poseidon's sake, where is she supposed to meet me?" I demanded.

"Not for Poseidon's sake, but for ours, young master." Duryattes skipped out of the way of my suddenly raised hand. He became serious. "I told the maid to bring her mistress to that maza stand over there." He pointed to a vendor cooking and selling hot maza bread from a small stand to our right.

We made our way cautiously over to the stand. The pancration competition had begun: the crowd was roaring, fists waving in the air. On the stadium floor I saw the monstrous Krelonan grappling with an athlete about two thirds his size. The huge Prienean wore a bloodthirsty grin as he battered his opponent's face with a hamlike fist, while holding him secure in a tight headlock. The smaller athlete was howling in protest.

The beautiful blonde form of Bilassa emerged from behind a pillar as we drew close to the maza stand, followed by her smirking maid. Gods above, she was gorgeous beyond description, a true representation of Aphrodite! Her snow-white cloak with its gleaming hood barely hid the profusion of golden curls peeking from around its edge, and her perfect body could not be disguised by the thin linen chiton beneath the unpinned outer garment. I closed my gaping mouth with a snap when Duryattes dug an elbow into my side, and bowed deeply to the vision in front of me.

"Mistress, I am Bias, son of Holicius and investigator of the magistrates of Priene," I muttered. "I would like to speak to you about the unfortunate matter of Tyrestes' death, if I may."

Bilassa turned angrily to her maid, who shrank back with a timorous smile.

"Virthisia, you said a handsome suitor wanted to meet me in secret," she scolded the slave in a high-pitched, breathless, little girl's voice. "I know about this Bias. He is neither handsome nor a suitor, I think!" She gestured at me dismissively with a perfect hand.

Now I admit I am not likely to win a contest with Adonis, but I believe I am well-enough proportioned in face and form to hold my own with most young Ionians. So I shrugged off this insult as an unfortunate error on the part of this earthly nymph, and attempted to salvage the situation.

"My lady, you misunderstand," I murmured smoothly, grasping the waving hand, as a bear might grab a swimming fish in a fast-running stream. She stared at her imprisoned hand in surprise.

"Your maid was not so far wrong," I continued. "Although I do want to speak to you about Tyrestes, I also may be considered a possible suitor, though obviously not as handsome as those you are used to!" I tightened my grip on her hand. Looking into my eyes, she smiled hesitantly.

"Oh, very well then, I shall let you woo me for a moment," she agreed softly. "But only for a moment. It's very improper, you know. What if my father should see us?" I kept the smile fixed on my not-so-handsome face.

"Um, yes, you're quite correct. As I said, you must have many handsome and athletic suitors vying for your father's permission to see you, indeed if not to wed you!" She had not disengaged her hand from mine, but let it lie there warm and still.

"Yes, there are many young men with their fathers who come to see my father, but I'm usually not allowed to talk to them." Her pouting lips drooped at the corners for an instant, and then curved up again. "But sometimes, like now, I can steal away for a moment, right under my brothers' noses!"

I looked around apprehensively to make sure that none of the three gigantic siblings were anywhere near us. Temporarily reassured, I asked her if she had spoken to my good friend Usthius yesterday at the chariot track.

"Indeed I did, noble Bias, with my maid's help," she answered innocently with a curiously blank look in those incredible eyes. "Did you know that he is the master of his own estate now that his illustrious brother Tyrestes has passed away? You wanted to ask me a question about Tyrestes, didn't you?"

Her smile was brilliant, the white even teeth gleaming between those perfect lips. I began to wonder if I was speaking to the right Bilassa. The one I had expected to meet was beautiful, but cold and calculating. This Bilassa appeared to be little more than a breathtaking child. Perhaps I was being played with here?

"Why, yes, Bilassa, I believe I did mention Tyrestes. He certainly was a tremendous athlete, wasn't he? But even great competitors want a beautiful and, if I may be so bold as to say, a wealthy wife to give them strong, handsome sons. Surely he was one of your suitors, just as his brother Usthius is now, eh?"

Her fine eyes clouded over as I spoke about Tyrestes, and she slowly pulled her hand from mine. She glanced over at Duryattes and her maid, who were speaking seriously to each other at a little distance from us.

"I am not sure I wish to speak about Tyrestes' efforts as a suitor. He was not a very honorable man, you know, in that way. And as for Usthius, I am afraid he is just a boy of eighteen. Even though he is master of his own estate, it will be quite a while before he weds, so my father tells me. I don't think he would be right for me."

"I always thought that Tyrestes was honorable in his dealings with fair ladies," I said, trying to coax more details from her. "He never spoke of any conquests he may have made or lonely wives he may have been seeing."

"Nevertheless, he didn't appreciate what I had to offer." She languidly fluffed her golden curls. "Other suitors have appreciated me more, I can assure you. I don't think he was a real gentleman, as my other suitors have been. He wasn't very considerate, and he was much too hasty." What in the name of Aphrodite of Cnidos was this girl talking about? Surely not what I *thought* she was talking about! Her eyes were now starting to roam about the crowd, as if searching for someone or something.

"What exactly do you mean, Bilassa, when you say he was not considerate and was too hasty?" To my surprise, she told me.

"When I am able to entertain a suitor without my father or brothers being present, I am accustomed to his making love gently and slowly, and giving me great pleasure," she explained clearly, as if to a great dolt. "My beauty and my father's wealth give me the choice of a suitor, not the other way around. Tyrestes was interested only in his own pleasure, not in mine. I am not accustomed to that, and didn't care for it." Her amazing eyes, wide and honestly childlike, stared directly into mine.

To say that I was absolutely speechless is far, far from the mark. The stadium fairly whirled about me as I absorbed these incredible statements, and I had to thrust a hand out against a pillar to steady myself. These were not the words of an aristocratic virgin, but rather those of a practiced courtesan! As from a great distance, I heard her concluding, "Of course, my father and brothers don't know about the adventures I have had with my suitors, or even about the many times I have entertained them unchaparoned. I am afraid they would be quite displeased if they discovered how I'm testing the water before jumping in! Virthisia helps me, you know, and they never guess!"

Bilassa apparently thought this a great joke, and her laughter tinkled merrily in the damp air. She looked at me earnestly after a moment.

"You are not so bad looking, now that I look at you closely, Bias." She touched my chest with the hand I had so recently held. "Perhaps we could meet later and see how you fare as a suitor?" As I looked about, searching for the right answer to the invitation, my blood froze as if I had been touched by the cold finger of Boreus, the north wind.

There, only about twenty rows down the stadium side toward the pancration competitions where they had been watching Krelonan crush his opponent, stood Bilassa's two Herculean brothers. As I was staring at them in horror, one turned and spotted his sister and me at the top of the stadium seating. His mouth opened in a conspicuous snarl, he elbowed his brother in the ribs, and started bearlike up the vertical slot that separates seating sections.

In a single heartbeat I grabbed Duryattes' arm, thrust him toward the stadium exit tunnel, and sprinted close on his heels. The boy turned in astonishment, spied the brothers lumbering up the stairway, and whirled about to race for the exit. He got there before I did, but that is only because I gave him a head start. If Hermes, the god of athletes, ever lent wings to a man's heels, he did then to mine. As I dashed down the tunnel exit to freedom, I heard the innocent girlish voice behind me.

"I am sure my father would approve of your family, and then you would have only to prove yourself to me!"

CHAPTER XVII

Bilassa's gargantuan protectors burst out of the tunnel entrance only a few lengths behind Duryattes and me.

As we ran down the cobbled street parallel to the stadium, they were lunging after us, shouting and gesturing. People passing us on their way to the games glanced at us in surprise or confusion, but nobody tried to stop us.

Now I believe I have mentioned that I am a pretty fair long distance runner, and Duryattes sprinted as only the very young can, so we should have easily eluded our pursuers. I do not think they recognized me, probably because of my dark cloak. They were calling "Hey, you!" and "Stop, whoreson!" behind us, but to my relief, I did not hear even one "Bias, you bastard!"

Note that I stated that we *should* have easily eluded our pursuers. They had fallen a good twenty lengths behind us, and their lumbering gait was perceptibly slowing as I darted another look over my shoulder. That was my mistake, since one really should not run forward while looking backward.

I faced front again just in time to dash headlong into a pair of donkeys crossing the street piled high with a basketweaver's goods.

Although the two beasts probably did not weigh any more than I did and I had a good deal of momentum built up, they were certainly more sure-footed than I. They did not go down, but I did. Caroming off the near animal, I bounced into his mate and was rewarded with a lusty kick to my backside. Propelled forcefully into the wall of a white-washed mud brick house, I collapsed onto the cobblestones, gasping like a fish out of water in its last moments. The donkeys, surprised and extremely annoyed, began bawling and kicking out at anything within reach, causing the unfortunate basketweaver to lose his grip and join me on the ground, cursing loudly at me and his asses. He and I both scrambled to get out of the way of the flying hooves, I rolling over and over to my right to bang back up against the house wall.

Needless to say, this accident allowed the twins from Hades to catch up to me. Thrusting a huge hand into my cloak front, the nearest one hauled me unceremoniously to my shaky feet, grasped my hair roughly with his other hand, and lifted me up bodily to shake me like a rat in the jaws of a slavering dog. This was probably not easy for him, as you will recall that my mother had recently given me a mourner's haircut, but he managed. My teeth rattled against each other like several pairs of divining bones in a oracle's hands.

"You were talking to our sister, you bastard!" roared the giant, who clutched me tightly. "Don't deny it! I saw you! Do not deny it!" He gave me a couple more prodigious shakes for good measure. I felt as if my head was going to snap off. Out of the corner of my eye I saw Duryattes sprinting away down the street, leaving me to my fate.

My attacker slammed me back against the wall, bouncing my head playfully a few times against the mud and brick and causing stars to dance across my vision. The second brother arrived just at this moment, and seized my cloak at the right shoulder. The first brother then shifted his hold to my left shoulder, and I was hauled up like a deer hung on a heavy tree branch to drain its lifeblood away.

"Stop, stop!" I croaked. "I am the priest of Poseidon, and the magistrates' investigator!" My heels beat a futile tattoo against the mud bricks.

"Being a priest will not help you, whoreson," grated the second sibling. "Who gave you permission to speak to Bilassa, eh? Answer that one, you cur!" He slapped my face several times for added emphasis as he spoke.

"I have the permission of the magistrates of Priene to speak to any citizen concerning the murder of the athlete Tyrestes!" I gurgled, clutching desperately at the front of my cloak to pull it away from my throat, where it was slowly strangling me. My vision was starting to gray out at the edges.

"Nobody but my father, Kreton, has the right to give anybody permission to speak with Bilassa!" bellowed Brother Number One furiously. The spittle flying from his lips splashed me in the face. The two giants gave me another head banging for good measure, and I felt my consciousness slipping away.

"No, I have a warrant!" I cried. "From the magistrates! Let me show you my warrant." I was desperate now, as I believed it was the intention of these two cyclops to do me some real harm. My ragged breathing sounded like the bellows of Zephyrus, that baleful wind who accompanied Boreus as he blew through the skies.

Miraculously, the shaking and banging stopped. I pried opened my eyes to see the two staring at me while they still held me upright so that my feet could not touch the cobbles.

"What do you mean, a warrant?" demanded Brother Number One. "A warrant to do what?"

"The magistrates!" I gasped hoarsely. "The magistrates have given me a warrant to question people about the death of Tyrestes! Let me down, and I will show it to you! Let me down!"

The gigantic pair eyed each other uncertainly for a moment, and then the first one nodded at the other. I was dropped abruptly into a heap at their sandalled feet, and then hauled up unceremoniously again by Brother Number Two.

"Let us see this so-called warrant," jeered Brother Number One.

"It is in my purse, here, in my purse," I babbled, searching frenziedly. I tore open the purse top and thrust the small piece of vellum at them. Brother Number One snatched it from my grasp, and I watched his lips moving as he read it.

By this time a small crowd had gathered around us, made up of curious gawkers and bored visitors. However, nobody lifted a hand to assist me; they all suspected this was a family matter, and family matters in Ionia were the business only of the two families involved.

Brother Number Two glared alternately at me and at his sibling. "Well, what does it say? What is it?"

Number One scratched his head and frowned.

"It *is* signed by the magistrates," he said. "It says that Bias of Priene has their authority to question anybody on the matter of the murder of Tyrestes, just as he said."

"The magistrates have no right to intrude on family prerogatives," snarled Number Two, keeping a tight grip on the front of my tunic and giving it a vicious twist. "Only Father can give permission for anybody to speak to Bilassa. He is probably just one of these bastards who's trying to bed Bilassa before Father gets her married off! He's just one of those trying to take advantage of her innocence!"

Number One's eyes narrowed as he glared at me. He dropped the warrant on the ground at my feet.

"I think you are right, brother," he growled, his hamlike fist drawing back in front of my face. "This piece of vellum is worth nothing. We'll teach this whoreson what happens when you insult an innocent daughter of Priene!" By the gods, I am finished, I thought, and struggled wildly in the grip of Number Two.

"That piece of vellum is worth a great deal!" a voice snapped angrily, and I saw a large hand on the end of a heavily muscled arm grasp Number One's shoulder from behind. "Let Bias go at once, do you hear?"

Number One swung around in surprise to confront the stern features of the magistrate Nolarion. Behind him, peeping timorously over his shoulder, I could see the face of Duryattes.

"Magistrate!" Number One blurted out in a shocked tone. "This is a family matter. We caught this fellow speaking to our sister without permission. He must be taught a lesson!"

"Are you deaf, you great idiot?" shouted Nolarion, shoving his face up to the startled visage of the speaking brother. "He has a warrant signed by the authorities of this city to investigate a murder. Look at his mourning clothing! Tyrestes died in his arms, and he is charged with dispensing the miasma infecting him and these games!"

Brother Number Two now noticed the black tunic beneath my cloak, and snatched his hand away as if it were singed. I sank back against the mud brick wall, gulping for air, and silently gave thanks to Poseidon for looking after his own.

Number One swung back to stare at me in my mourning clothing, and then at the warrant that Nolarion had picked up and was shaking in the giant's face.

"Defy this warrant, and I will have you apprehended for interfering with the government of this city," he threatened, waving it back and forth. The giant's eyes followed the document from side to side and then he reluctantly stepped away.

"Very well, Magistrate," he growled. "But know this. I will speak to my father about your warrant and your authority. This is a family matter!" He locked his gaze on my somewhat battered visage. "And you," he snarled. "Don't speak to my sister again, warrant or not. She is not to be bothered by any unmarried man. She is too innocent for the likes of you, priest or investigator or whatever!" He spat angrily onto the cobbles by my feet, glared one last time at the big magistrate, and stalked off, followed by the protesting and bewildered Brother Number Two. Nolarion turned to me in anger.

"Are you mad, Bias? That warrant is worth only what an individual citizen thinks it is worth. I would hope that you know that. What in Poseidon's name do you think you were doing, talking to a single woman without permission?" I struggled to stand upright, and began to straighten my clothing.

"I spoke to Kreton's daughter Bilassa because I believe she may have been involved in the murder," I said. "I thought you and the other magistrates issued me that warrant in order to find a murderer. I cannot do that if I don't obtain facts and opinions by talking to people."

Nolarion considered me fiercely for a moment. "You must know that you can't flout the rules of our society with impunity, warrant or not. You should have asked Kreton for permission to talk to his daughter."

"If I had done that, the answer would have been 'no' or else I would have had to speak to her in the presence of a brother or a loyal slave. I would have learned nothing."

"And what did you learn?" inquired the magistrate, his curiosity overcoming his annoyance with me. "Is she involved with the murder?"

"I don't believe so. I honestly believe she does not have the intelligence to have helped to plan these crimes." I could have added that she also had the morals of a street whore, but of course I didn't.

"Well, if nothing else, that eliminates one of your possible suspects." Nolarion tugged at his luxuriant black beard, and sighed gustily. "What will you do next in your plan?" He peered at me expectantly from under bushy brows. Although I knew what I planned to do next, which was speak to Usthius, I suddenly did not want him to know. I do not know why I felt this way—I simply did.

"I do not know what to do next," I lied, looking straight into those dark eyes. "I think I may go to the baths and steam some of the pain from my head and shoulders!"

He nodded, told me to be more prudent, and turned to go.

"Thank you for your intervention, Magistrate. I do not like to think of what would have happened if you had not been near here."

"I was not, Bias," he said, stopping to look back at me. "Your servant ran into the stadium and told me that you were in mortal danger. You are in his debt, not mine." He walked swiftly back to the stadium.

Duryattes had been waiting in silent expectation by the wall to my side. He looked at me in what I took to be amusement, but did not so much as twitch his mouth in the beginnings of a smile.

"I wish to thank you, Duryattes," I said carefully. This admission did not come easily to me. "You acted swiftly and decisively. I must admit that I initially did you the injustice of thinking you had run away, but I can see that I was mistaken. You acted in the best tradition of the house of Holicius."

He grinned and bowed slightly.

"Young master, I admit I did consider running away for an instant when the two giants were upon us, but I quickly thought better of it. My father, Dryses, would never have forgiven me if I had let harm befall the heir of the house of Holicius!"

I grinned back at him, and reached up to rub the back of my aching head.

CHAPTER XVIII

I CAME TO THE HASTY CONCLUSION that a few hours in the public baths would serve me better than watching the morning's remaining events. I still planned to see Usthius either before or after the horse racing that afternoon, but my initial desire to watch the long race had evaporated with my present need to soothe my battered body in the hot water of the baths.

Duryattes was dispatched to the hippodrome to try and arrange a meeting between Usthius and me through the medium of a personal servant. Duryattes assured me that he was a great friend of this particular slave, and would have no trouble in setting up this rendezvous. Whistling a rousing tune from one of the recent popular comedies of the city, my cheerful companion sauntered away down the cobbled street.

As for me, I headed off in the opposite direction for the public baths, wincing and full of complaints. My head still ached, but after carefully taking stock of the rest of my body, I decided that I was fortunate to have gotten away with only the slight injuries that I suffered.

Even with the events continuing in the stadium, the streets were still bustling with sellers, buyers, theater goers, musicians, street entertainers, and the like, all smiling, chatting, pushing, and generally enjoying themselves. It took me some little time to maneuver my way to the entrance of the baths building, though it was only a short distance down the stadium lane.

Priene has quite impressive public baths, you know, although obviously nothing like the monstrous edifices in Miletus or Athens. Two rows of tall white pillars stretched across the façade of the building for about fifteen paces; the portico led to a large room, or andron, filled with couches and chairs. Here one could drink, snack, and discuss the events of the day without having to go into the baths proper. It was nearly empty at the moment with most of its usual patrons at the games, but two old men, accompanied by youthful male admirers, sat chattering away happily in the far corner and waved to me as I went from the andron into the changing room.

I doffed my cloak and somber black tunic, hung them on a peg to be brushed and dusted by one of the slaves who handed me a linen towel, and padded off through the right hand door to the hot room.

The hot room was aptly named for two reasons. First, it had a huge native stone hearth against one wall, where a fire was kept blazing during all hours that the baths were open. Even in the winter this kept the room pleasantly warm, but in the late spring, summer, or early autumn, the place was like the realm of Hades. Beads of sweat immediately popped out all over my body, as I entered the room through the thick curtain which retained the heat and moisture.

Secondly, the room had a small rock pool in the center constantly replenished by a thin stream of hot water. This was ingeniously accomplished by continuous heating of water in large kettles just on the other side of the hot room's outer wall. Several slaves fed the fires constantly to maintain a low flame under the kettles. The water flowed out of the kettles through a spout in the wall and down a tiled tunnel to the pool, and out again through a tunnel on the other side. One could simply sit in the hot pool, which was the length and breadth of two tall men, and relax in the soothing swirl of water. I promptly did just that, there being no one else in the room. I must tell you, however, that I believe the fire-tending slaves were taking advantage of the lack of patrons, because the water was not nearly as hot as it should have been.

At any rate I was able to soak for some time in the tepid liquid, considering my situation and wondering how to proceed with Usthius when I found him. I liked the idea of speaking to him, as the family's representative, about Risalla's future; and that was the approach I believed least likely to end in another physical contest for which I was woefully unprepared. Not to say that I could not have taken Usthius if I wished, you understand. But not at that moment.

Arising from the tiled pool with a sigh, I sat on one of the marble benches in the hot room and dipped into a large jug of warm olive oil, rubbing it into my skin and muscles with a heavy hand. Again, I thought ruefully that if I had come here in the evening after the athletic events of the day, I would have had the services of a half-dozen slaves adept at kneading the oil into tired arms and legs. Ah, well.

Scraping off the oil with a bronze strigel, I left the hot room and entered the cold room. It also had a hearth on one wall, not so large as the monster in the hot room, but at this time of year the fire was not even lit. The room was pleasantly cool because a large amount of marble covered the floors and walls, and because of the tiled pool of cold water in the center of the room. When I say this water was cold, I mean it was like the water beneath the covering of ice in a pond on a winter's day. The cold room's pool was fed directly by an underground spring, and so was constantly replenished by a steady stream of icy liquid.

The pool was occupied by a cheerful elder, who was splashing himself gleefully with the icy water. He grinned at me as I edged up to the rim and then stepped off into the depths with my eyes closed. Actually, it was not very deep, only about half a man's length, but the shock to the system made it feel as if one had jumped into the sea in mid-winter. I shouted involuntarily as my head broke water, and leaped out immediately, spluttering and cursing. This was the cause of much amusement to the elderly gentleman, as he stood splashing in the corner of the pool. Clambering to my feet at the pool's edge, I enjoyed sharing a moment of laughter with him.

Feeling much refreshed, I left the old man chuckling contentedly in the pool, and made my way to the final door, which led back into the changing room. Donning my garments, which I noted were *not* dusted and brushed very well, I walked back through the andron, waved cheerfully at the two elders still chatting in the corner, and headed toward the hippodrome to find my loyal Duryattes and the mysterious Usthius.

As I wended my way, I thought about my conversation with the beautiful Bilassa. What possible reason could she have for killing either of the two athletes? My suspicions about her were founded on the surmise that she may have been grievously insulted by a lover's indiscretions or change of heart. If I correctly interpreted her remarks to me, that was about as likely as Pan being insulted because he was accused of seducing too many nymphs! And I could not really believe that she was capable of planning two complicated murders.

No, I decided morosely that I could eliminate Bilassa as an active member of any plot to destroy the athletes. Of course, there was the possibility that Usthius could have done it without her knowledge because of his desire for her. Farfetched, you say? Maybe so, but one could never tell about these things.

The crowd was beginning to thicken now on the street leading to the hippodrome on the outskirts of the city. By listening to snatches of conversation I deduced that with Habiliates gone, a lithe boy from Samos had come from behind to win the long race, and Krelonan had rated highly in the initial standings of the pancration fighting event. No surprise there. Endemion had scored well in the long jump and would be participating in the finals of that event tomorrow. I reflected that he would have to dig deep within himself to win most or all of the events in which he was a finalist tomorrow, and then still remain viable for the pentathlon on the next and final day. After all, his father had achieved the same accomplishment twenty years before. Like father, like son? Or were the son's chances being improved by a judicious killing here and there?

As I drew near the hippodrome, Duryattes came skipping over to my side from behind some rocks.

"Thank the gods you got here in time, young master," he panted, dancing back and forth. "The noble Usthius has been informed that you are here to speak to him about your sister and will meet with you before the race!"

"It looks as if we have an hour or so." I squinted at the sun's position in the overcast sky. "Come, let us find something to eat, and then I will meet with our next suspect." Duryattes' eyes shone brightly at the prospect, and together we purchased and ate olives, grapes, and maza bread, washed down with cold spring water.

We found Usthius in one of the horse corrals on the far side of the hippodrome, where he and his servant were currying and grooming a magnificent black stallion. They were tying strings of ribbons in the animal's braided mane and tail, and polishing his hooves with black dye and olive oil. Our target was dressed in his black tunic, much like mine, but I noticed again that his hair had not been sheared nearly as short as mine. My overzealous mother or his statement of his true feelings toward his dead brother?

"Greetings, Usthius," I spoke loudly as we came up to him. "I thank you for agreeing to speak with me before the race. I do not see Euphemius here. Surely he is the owner of this marvelous beast?"

"Euphemius is making wagers at the track. We are to join him there with the horse shortly. I understand that you wish to speak to me about your sister, Risalla?" He was about my height, but slim and boyish with a petulant feminine face and long delicate hands. He had pale, almost washed-out eyes, and his lips were too full for his thin face. He was not tanned and overtly muscular like his brother Tyrestes, but gave the impression of tension coiled within, like a whip before it is snapped over the heads of a racing chariot team.

"That is true," I confirmed, leaning casually against a corral post. He muttered a few words to his groom about continuing the horse's preparations and motioned for me to follow him to a small rock outcropping outside the corral. Duryattes stayed where he was, talking to the groom.

"Are you here officially at the behest of your father?" Usthius asked hesitantly. I thought I detected a hint of nervousness in his manner. All to the good.

"No, no, nothing like that. Let us say that I am here to look after Risalla's best interests before my father learns about your dalliances with her." I hardened my voice as I spoke the last four words.

"Dalliances?" he sputtered, taken aback. Alarm flared in his pale eyes. "Surely you speak too harshly, noble Bias. I haven't dallied with your sister. Why, look at me! I'm much too young to wed."

"Perhaps we are not speaking of wedding." I moved toward him menacingly. "Risalla has told me that you have spoken to her several times in the past months, and your language bordered very much on the improper the last time at the opening ceremonies of the games. What do you say to that, eh?"

Usthius stepped back from me.

"What have you done with my sister, you cur, and what are your intentions?" I snarled, grabbing at the front of his tunic. He stumbled back again, tripped over a projecting root, and sat down in the dust with a thump.

"I have done nothing improper, Bias!" He scrambled to his feet, fear widening those strange eyes. "You must believe me! We have spoken a few times, but that's all. I know that I should have asked you or your father's permission to speak to her, but it happened innocently in the agora. I have done nothing else, nor do I intend to!"

"That is not what Risalla claims," I countered, circling around the rocks to close the distance between us. He did the same in the opposite direction, so that, to an onlooker, we must have looked like two boxers circling in a ring.

"Let me explain," he pleaded, holding his hands up in front of him. We stopped circling and stared at each other over the boulder between us.

It was ironic, really, my pretending to play the same role the giant brothers of Bilassa had played several hours before. I almost chuckled, but caught myself in time.

"Well, explain then!" I demanded and added a curse for effect.

"We only talked about possibilities," he said. "Why, I was not even the head of my household then. How could I have proposed anything to Risalla?"

"Perhaps even then you had plans to be the head of your family, eh, Usthius?" I whispered harshly. "It is well known that you and Tyrestes were not close and disagreed about many things. How much easier for you to seduce innocent girls like my sister with the lying promise of an estate."

"Had plans to be the head of my family?" Usthius repeated in confusion. "What do you mean?"

"I mean that you could easily try to sway Risalla into your bed by promising that she would become the mistress of your estate! Just as you could persuade Bilassa, eh, you dog?"

His head snapped back as if I had struck him. He glanced wildly about as if contemplating flight, and I thought for a moment that he might actually run. But his next words surprised me.

"Are you completely mad, Bias?" he demanded, staring at me and clenching his fists. "Are you accusing me of murdering my brother to get my estate?" He lifted his eyes to the heavens and snickered in disdain. I must admit I was taken aback by his reaction.

"What in the name of Poseidon are you laughing at?" I shouted. "You are the mad one here, not I!"

His laughter subsided as quickly as it had erupted, and his eyes were wide and angry, as he snarled at me.

"You fool! You amateur! Do you have any idea of the state of my land? I am virtually without a stater! Why do you think I'm riding for Euphemius in this horse race? Why do you think I rode in that insane chariot race yesterday?"

"Why, to gain the glory of the victory in your brother's place," I blurted out. "It's well known that you were jealous of him!"

"I was what?" he asked in an amazed tone. "I was jealous of him? You *are* mad! I am riding in these races because Euphemius is paying me, you idiot. I wouldn't take part in these dangerous races otherwise!"

I was absolutely dumbfounded. I had never heard of such a thing in my entire life. Paying him! Paying him to ride in the great games!

"Euphemius knew I was the only one beside Tyrestes who could halfway handle his crazy horses," Usthius went on. "I refused to have anything to do with the races until he offered me a tidy sum to participate. He wants to win a race badly, and I am his only chance, though not much of a chance,

I admit. But I must have that money. My brother left the estate with virtually nothing except the land and a broken-down house. I have no flocks, no horses, no grapes, nothing!"

He paused for breath, and then rushed on.

"And as for Bilassa, the other part of your wild accusation, she has the morals of a street slut. She approached me yesterday as a substitute for Tyrestes, and when I told her that her actions were not proper, she laughed at me and called me a sexless dolt. She even made a grab under my tunic, if you believe it, and jeered at me when I shied away! She is even less moral than Risalla!"

That last sentence had obviously been unintentional, for as soon as the words left his mouth, he clamped his teeth shut with an audible click and whirled to try and escape. Of course, I could not let him get away with this accusation, be it true or not. I caught the neck of his tunic with my outstretched hand even as he turned, and clubbed him on his ear with a clenched fist.

He howled as if the Nemean Lion were on him, and struck out wildly with both fists, pummeling me randomly about the head and shoulders. I hung onto him mercilessly despite the blows and struck him hard several times, until at last he collapsed in the dirt, sobbing and wiping a bloody nose.

"I have done nothing," he wept bitterly, as I stood over him with my fists still bunched. "I want nothing to do with Risalla or Bilassa. Gods above, I am only eighteen and have nothing to offer anybody. I must accept money for riding in these races just to try and pay off my brother's creditors. Let me alone, for Poseidon's sake!" He sat there in the dust, big tears welling out of his eyes and mingling with the blood and mucus running out of his nose.

What a contemptible character, I thought. Not even Risalla or the sluttish beautiful Bilassa would want to have anything to do with him. I felt ashamed that I had laid hands on him, even though I had little choice under the circumstances.

"Listen, you cur," I hissed, standing over him like a boxer in the games staring at a downed opponent. "Don't ever speak to my sister again, do you hear? You're a piece of sheep dung who is not fit to hold his brother's cast-off sandals, much less own his estate."

It only occurred to me some moments later, as I walked away with Duryattes at my side, that I had indeed treated him exactly as the brothers of Bilassa had treated me. Ah, well, one acts very differently when the sandal is on the other foot, eh? I longed to be finished with the whole sordid business.

CHAPTER XIX

I HAD NO INTEREST IN staying to watch Usthius win or lose in the horse race, so I walked slowly back into the city. I was in a foul mood, disgusted both with Usthius and my own actions. The narrow, cobbled streets with their stone and mud houses seemed to mock me as I moved along, oblivious to the shouts and laughter of the many citizens and visitors who streamed in the opposite direction toward the hippodrome. Was my own mind and perception as narrow as some of the side streets I passed, streets so tight that three men could scarce walk abreast down them? Was I now at the point of my investigation, where still having no idea who the murderer was, I was reduced to being assaulted or assaulting other people? I sent a silent message to Poseidon to give me a little assistance.

Duryattes was no help at all. He was mightily interested in horses, it transpired, and whined about not being able to stay for the race. His complaints were interspersed with admiring comments about the way I had physically handled Usthius, an act for which I felt a nagging sense of shame. I finally snapped at him to be quiet, and his commentary ended abruptly in a surprised silence.

After a good two hours of wandering this way and that, lost in morose thoughts, I noted with little enthusiasm that I was back near the southern entrance of the stadium. There were still a large number of people going in and out. Most of the ones going out probably did not care for horse racing. I presumed my father and the girls would be at the hippodrome, since Holicius *did* care for horse racing, but I decided to remain within the stadium and wait for the return of the main crowd to see the initial discus competition. Duryattes and I entered through the covered stadium tunnel into the sparsely filled stands, and I blinked several times as a short, stocky man some twenty rows down waved at me.

It was Polearchus the Miletian, the kinsman of the dead Habiliates. He waved again to make certain he had caught my attention, and then motioned me toward him. Oh, well, I thought wearily with a shrug, perhaps it is better to be with somebody than to sulk by oneself. I descended the stepped walkway to where the little Miletian stood waiting.

"Greetings, Bias," he said, as I approached. He held out his hand, which I grasped at the wrist, and gave me a small, grim smile. Motioning for me to sit down, he plopped back down himself and poured two cups of wine from a jug he had sitting at his feet.

"If you want a drink of decent wine, you have to bring your own," he commented dryly as he handed me a cup. "This is from Chios, although not their best. Still, it's better than the rotgut that the wine sellers are hawking hereabouts." I dipped my cup at him and took a long swallow. Ah, it was good, mellow and delightful. I heaved a conspicuous sigh.

"How goes your inquiries into the death of the two young men?" Polearchus asked softly, sipping the excellent wine. I stared down into my cup at the rich purple liquid swirling within.

"I have never done anything like this before. I have spoken with many people and have learned many facts, but none of them seem to fit together into a coherent whole. It is like a child's wooden puzzle, where the pieces all fit together, but I don't know where to place the first piece." I gestured helplessly. Polearchus nodded slowly, still sipping from his cup.

"Perhaps it would help you to lay out everything you know to someone who is neither too close nor too far from the whole affair? I myself do not know all the 'facts' that you have gathered, and I'm not a Prienean, so I'm not predisposed to suspect anybody in particular. My interest is entirely personal, of course, but I would very much like the murderer to be caught rather than have to make my announcement the day after tomorrow." He looked at me sideways from under lowered brows and smiled slightly again. I began to like this small man with his triangular beard and considered his advice.

"I think that perhaps you are correct," I admitted at length. "You may be able to see something as an outsider that I have missed. I certainly cannot think of anything else I can do to proceed at the moment."

"Good man," he said softly with his ghost of a smile. "Begin anywhere you wish and I shall listen carefully until you are finished."

Where to begin? I decided that a chronological recitation would do as well as any and was about to begin, when a drunken citizen stumbled down the walkway to my right and knocked my wine cup out of my hands. I clambered to my feet, but my unintentional assailant had already reeled further down the aisle, so I turned ruefully to my companion instead.

"The stadium is filling up again in preparation for the discus throwing," I explained apologetically. "This may not be the time or place for a long recital on my part." Polearchus, who was wiping wine off his sandalled feet, looked up at me and nodded.

"I think you're right about the place, but not about the time. Why don't we go to my tents along the bank of the river south of the hippodrome, and speak further there? It will be quiet there now in the afternoon. I have some excellent wine and food, and Machus, my carpenter and chariot maker, is there. He is a clever fellow, and with two of us listening instead of one, we may be able to see a glimmer of light for you somewhere in your darkness. Do you particularly want to stay here to view the discus throwing?"

I did not, and was suddenly grateful to the little Miletian for his friendliness and sensible suggestions. I agreed to his proposal immediately, and we rose to go to his home away from home. I turned to Duryattes, who had been standing close by, obviously trying desperately to hear our conversation while seeming disinterested.

"Duryattes, you stay here and tell my father when he returns that I have gone with the noble Polearchus to his tents. I will go back to the house from there sometime tonight." Duryattes watched unhappily as I followed the Miletian up the aisle to the stadium exit.

Polearchus and I strolled down the slanting streets toward the riverfront, engaging in polite conversation about the games, but deliberately not speaking about the crimes. He had business to conduct at several shops along the way, and politely asked if I would mind if he combined this present task with others. I said of course not, so it was several hours before we arrived at the beginning of the flat expanse of land on the river's edge upon which his tents reared themselves in the middle of a virtual tent city. It was early evening by now, and my stomach was beginning to complain with gurgles and growls about how I had been ignoring it.

"I beg your pardon, Polearchus," I mumbled. "I had only a few grapes and olives for deipnon. We should stop, and I will buy us some food."

"Nonsense, Bias! I told you I have good food and wine at my tents, and so I do. We are almost there. We'll eat before you tell me your suspicions in this tragic affair."

I followed through the tiny temporary lanes past tents and shacks of every imaginable size, shape, and color. In this early evening time, as Helios was just beginning to urge the sun's horses below the horizon, the shades of color were muted and the shadows caused by erect poles, barrels, carts, and hanging laundry were starting to lengthen. Ropes and guy lines ran every which way, and I reflected wryly to myself that you could easily throttle yourself, if you tried to play the children's game of tag in this rabbit warren.

Most of the inhabitants of this makeshift town were at the stadium, although I thought they should be coming home soon, since the discus throwing event must be about over in the growing twilight. There were a few people about: women starting meals over braziers, a group of children running about in noisy abandon even at this hour, and slaves and servants guarding their masters' temporary homes. The overhanging gray clouds had begun to drizzle again, causing most of the adults to be swathed in cloaks with hoods or hats.

"Here is my kingdom by your city," announced Polearchus, stopping in front of a cluster of tents. He swept his arm toward an area of four square-shaped structures.

"They are made with poles and tent coverings that we brought from Miletus in a wagon. I have travelled up and down the length of Ionia in the service of the Miletian Assembly and decided several years ago that it was foolish to depend on what you could find in the local area for your comfort." He strode toward the largest of the four strange-looking tents, and called out for Machus.

Nobody appeared.

"Maybe he is out buying food for our dorpon meal." Polearchus flung aside the hanging cloth that served as the door to the tent. "Although I thought we had enough food for today. Ho, Machus, are you in there?"

He thrust his head inside the tent, peering around its dark interior, and I heard him grunt in surprise.

"Machus, what in the name of Apollo are you doing? What is. . . ." His voice trailed off as he moved inside. I stuck my head inside the opening to see him hurrying in the gloom toward a form lying on the floor near the back of the tent. There were large bales and bundles scattered about the interior, and I had a fleeting thought that the Miletian must be conducting a great deal of business in addition to attending the athletic contests.

It was the last coherent thought I had for several moments, because my head abruptly exploded in pain.

I have no way of telling how much time slipped by before I became conscious of my surroundings, but I think it was only an instant or two. I found myself lying face down, my cheek pressed against a small, rough stone in the packed dirt floor. I heard what sounded like struggling close by, and then a muffled shriek, quickly chopped off. I tried to lift my head, which felt very heavy, not my usual head at all. I was rewarded for this effort by an incredible spear of pain below and to the rear of my right ear, which forced me back to the floor with a jolt.

Vaguely I noted a heavily swathed figure moving about in the gloom. Must be Polearchus, I thought. But why was I on the floor, and where had this intense agony come from? I reached back fumbling at the right side of my head and felt warm liquid on my fingers. Blood, I thought incredulously, what is happening here?

In another corner of the tent was a low brazier. I saw the figure reach into the bowl with a pair of bronze tongs and stir the sleeping coals. Selecting a live one, he hesitated for a moment, and then picked up an olive oil jug, and poured the olive oil over a bundle of clothing nearby. I really must get up, I told myself, but my body refused to cooperate, only my bloodied hand scrabbled ineffectually at the dirt floor.

The figure thrust the tongs holding the live coal against the oil-soaked rags, watching as the bundle smoldered briefly and then burst into flames. He dropped the tongs, and moved in a scuttling sideways fashion to stand over me. Polearchus, I thought wildly, what are you doing? Help me up!

Instead, the figure swung back a foot and kicked me soundly in the ribs. My breath gushed out of my lungs in a rush as new agony erupted in my side! The figure seemed to consider the situation for a moment, gave me another vicious kick for good measure, and then turned to stride out of the tent into the lighter grayness outside. Doubled up in an anguished ball, all I could see was that my assailant waited for an instant in the doorway, and then the hooded form was gone.

I lay on the hard-packed earth and fought to draw air into my tortured lungs. I drew in several shaky breaths amidst considerable pain, and then turned my head back towards the rear of the tent. Terror gripped my brain, forcing its way through the pain!

The bundle of clothing was burning brightly, and another bundle next to it now caught as well. Get up, Bias you idiot, I screamed to myself, before everything in this tent goes up in flames!

This time my battered body must have received the message, because I rolled slightly to my side and managed to sit up. But the effort exhausted me, and I sat propped against a bale by the door of the tent, staring stupidly at the fire. The hungry flames had now spread to the far wall of the cloth structure and began to lick up the sides toward the ceiling. The smoke reached me in a long, curling tendril, and I sucked it in, coughing roughly and redoubling the agony from my ribs. Move, I must move!

The smoke thickened rapidly, billowing out from the flaming bundles of trade goods in the big tent. The heat became terrific, sapping my strength. I tried to stand, gave up the idea quickly and began to crawl toward the tent entrance. The flames were lapping at my heels, and I thought I could feel them fondling my feet, singing the hair of my calves. Poseidon, help me! Clutching the edges of the opening, I pulled myself halfway out of the tent into the damp grass outside. Rolling over, I beat weakly at my smoldering sandals with my hands and looked up to see the entire front of the structure blazing above me.

Suddenly, hands grasped me under my arms and jerked me unceremoniously backwards. I slid along the wet ground, my heels dragging in the mud, until I was four or five lengths from the burning tent. Lying in the misty drizzle I saw my rescuer shoot me a look of concern and turn abruptly away to join several other men flinging water on the conflagration. There was a great deal of shouting and noise. At that point my mind said, enough is enough, and blackness washed over me.

I do not know how long I lay there in the cold mud, as the fire burned through a good tenth of that tent city. When I awoke I was lying under a flap of cloth, the rain dripping through onto my chilled form and the sun completely gone. I fluttered a hand up to gingerly touch my head, which seemed to be a temporary home for the forge of Hephaestus, and discovered that it had at least stopped bleeding. Very carefully sitting up, I peered around me.

Torches and smoldering remnants of burnt tents and shacks provided some light, transforming the scene into a realistic version of the outskirts of Hades. Smoke and mist had combined to shroud the whole area in grayness, through which figures moved, talking loudly to each other. The smell of burnt meat permeated the air, as if we were back at the sacrificial barbecue of the Panionion. I started with surprise when a face suddenly loomed up before me.

"Are you all right then, sir?" the face asked. "I thought the fire might have finished you off, eh?"

"Are you the one who pulled me from the tent?" I croaked, my throat seared and my voice almost unrecognizable. I noted his rough tunic and unkempt hair. Somebody's servant.

"Yes, sir, that was me," he affirmed with a grim smile. "Fire almost had you, didn't it? Let's see if you can stand, eh?" He stepped forward, grasped me roughly under the arms again, and hoisted me none too gently to my feet. I swayed there for several moments in his arms.

"My thanks for saving me," I gasped, regarding the scene about me with shock and dismay. All around were the blackened remains of the temporary homes, and people were scurrying or trudging here and there, trying to make some order out of the chaos. My benefactor glanced about.

"Could have been much worse without the rain," he commented, spitting abruptly on the ground. "Twenty or so tents have gone, but luckily most of the people were still coming back from the stadium. My master's tents made it through all right." He gestured with a shrug toward an impressive set of tents to our right.

When he released me to see if I could stand on my own, I did not immediately collapse on the ground. My head and ribs hurt abominably, but I was undoubtedly lucky to be alive and relatively unburnt. I glanced down at my legs, noting with detached interest that much of the hair had been singed off my calves and that the skin there smarted as if badly sunburned. Lucky indeed.

"I was a guest of Polearchus of Miletus," I said to the burly servant, who had turned to walk away back to his master's area now that I was apparently mobile. "Have you seen him about?"

The man turned back to me.

"Polearchus is dead, sir. He and his slave Machus. They were killed in the fire. Whatever goddess wept today in the heavens smiled on you, eh? Without her tears of rain, you and many others might be waking up in the underworld."

CHAPTER XX

I STAYED AT THE DEVASTATED site of the tent city for about an hour, gathering my strength for the walk back uphill to the city proper and steeling myself for a look at the two dead bodies. The helpful servant brought me a cup of heady wine at his master's bequest, which I sipped gingerly. Many people were now milling about, having arrived from the stadium after the final event of the day. Those whose property had been destroyed or damaged could be heard cursing or wailing. The destruction would undoubtedly have been much worse if it were not for the drizzling rain. It was certainly bad enough as it was, and the news filtered through the tent city that three or four other poor souls had perished in the conflagration.

I finally worked up enough courage to approach the bodies of Polearchus and Machus where they lay covered by a cloth. Bending over to pull away the cloth immediately set the hammer and anvil in my head to banging again, so I knelt on the wet ground to inspect the corpses.

"May I ask who you are, sir?" a voice spoke behind me. A well-dressed middleaged man was standing looking down at me.

"Merely an acquaintance of Polearchus," I said. "I had come back with him to his tents to share some wine, food, and conversation."

"Ah, well, I am from Miletus, like most of the people in this part of the tent city. I have known Polearchus many years. We will see that his body is brought back to Miletus for burial. These games have been nothing but bad luck for him and his family. You know that his nephew, Habiliates, was killed in the chariot race?"

"Had you spoken to him since his nephew's unfortunate death?" I hoped my tone was deceptively innocent.

"Yes, just this morning, as a matter of fact. He was very upset about the death. He hinted a few times that he believed it may not have been an accident at all, but I don't see how that could be, do you? I mean, after all, chariot racing is a risky business. People get killed and injured all the time. No, I think he was simply distraught behind his calm exterior, and could not accept that the gods had allowed Habiliates to pass away before he could fulfill his glorious destiny of winning the games for Miletus."

The man pulled the cloth over the corpses, bade me farewell, and went back toward his own tents. I stared after him for a moment, thinking about what he had just told me. If all Polearchus had done was hint to his fellow Miletians that the death of Habiliates was deliberate, then no one would know that a guestslaying had occurred. He had apparently kept the information to himself, and with both him and his servant dead, the miasma that enveloped the city would remain unknown and unseen.

Except that now I knew there had been three guestslayings, not one. The cloaked figure in Polearchus' tent had finished the Miletian aristocrat, as well as his servant. It simply could not have been a coincidence, the two being killed by some robber or vagabond, could it? Well, I supposed that odder things had happened, but no, the stakes were too high. These two murders, for that is what they were, had to be connected to the deaths of Tyrestes and Habiliates.

And to top it all, the cloaked figure had obviously meant the minor priest of Poseidon to perish in the flames as well. My aching head and ribs attested to that, as well as my seared calves and sore lungs. It was simply a case of the gods smiling on me, while they frowned on Polearchus and Machus. The final frown.

My head was pounding ferociously. I headed back up the narrow, slanting streets, trudging wearily out of the tent city. I was no longer hungry, feeling rather ill, so I decided to visit the baths again and get cleaned up.

It was still early in the evening, though it seemed to me that many hours had passed; this was undoubtedly the longest day of my life. The baths were filled with patrons, as I knew they would be, now that the games had ended for the day. Dozens of citizens and visitors were clustered in the big andron room off the pillared entrance, chattering, drinking, and having a fine old time. Asses, I thought sourly, as I edged through the andron toward the changing room door while several aristocrats stared in disapproval at my disheveled appearance. I quickly shed my singed and muddy mourning garments into the arms of a shocked slave, who looked at them and me in some dismay, wondering, no doubt, how he was ever going to make them presentable. But he bowed and scuttled out a side door, where I knew there was a tub of soapy water waiting for my clothes.

The hot room was not as filled with patrons as the andron, but at least ten men were there, luxuriating in the hot pool or lazing around on the marble benches being massaged and oiled by a half dozen slaves. Nobody I knew, thank the gods. A couple of them glanced at me quickly, noting the mud, blood, and growing bruises.

"Rough day in the athletics today, eh?" one of them quipped from his perch on a nearby bench. He winced as a slave kneaded his shoulders. "Looks like you got in over your head in the pancration or boxing?" I nodded at him, cutting off further conversation, and motioned to a slave to wash me down with a hot sponge, so that I could climb into the hot pool. He carefully sponged me down, scraped off the worst of the dirt with a bronze strigel, and helped me into the pool. The water was scalding hot this time, the steam rising into the overheated air. I inched into it carefully, and settled myself gratefully on the marble lip set in the water.

"Sir, if you desire, we have an iatros physician standing by, because of the games, who can examine your wound," said the slave softly in my ear, as I eased into the water. I agreed, and he hurried away to fetch the follower of Aesclepius.

A short while later, he returned with a small, rotund man who clucked impatiently at the sight of me. When I assured him that my head wound was probably the only injury he could assist me with, he examined the lump behind my ear. Bathing it with a sponge dipped in vinegar set it to smarting, but he pronounced it a minor injury that did not need sewing. When he saw me catch my breath several times, he insisted on prodding and poking my ribs with a pudgy finger. He then announced to the interested onlookers that I had several cracked ribs. He advised me to bind my chest tightly upon returning home, and leave the binding on underneath my tunic for at least one month. The iatros then accepted ten stater from my purse and bustled out of the room.

Sighing, I resettled myself in the pool to relax my battered muscles.

My slightly burned legs could not take much of the hot water, however, and began to protest vehemently. I thought the cold pool might help the pain a little.

I went through the covered door into the cooler air of the cold room where a dozen or so occupants were splashing in the cold water or rubbing themselves down with olive oil to be scraped off with a strigel. It was apparent they were all athletes—all of them had splendid physiques marred with bruises and scrapes here and there, and were chattering animatedly among themselves about the day's contests. In the far corner next to the small hearth, Usthius sat with a cup in his hand, smiling contentedly. His look of happiness changed instantly to one of apprehension when I appeared in the doorway. On a bench next to him two other competitors relaxed, laughing with each other. They were Endemion and Mycrustes, and enthusiastically waved me over when they spotted me. I shuffled over to their bench and accepted a kylix of wine from Mycrustes. Perching on the edge of the cold pool, I lowered my smarting legs into the chilly water. Immediately my limbs ceased their vociferous protests, and thanked me for my solicitude.

"Ho, Bias!" Mycrustes greeted me loudly. "You must congratulate us. Endemion and I have both qualified for the finals tomorrow in the discus, and young Usthius here actually won the horse race for Priene!" Endemion grinned broadly and punched Mycrustes on the shoulder, and Usthius produced a hesitant smile.

"Congratulations, indeed, then," I answered warmly. "Well done, all of you, especially you, Usthius." A dark flush spread over his face.

"Euphemius is very pleased," he muttered, taking a gulp of his wine.

"I should say he is," boomed out Mycrustes. "I don't think he will take off that crown of laurel leaves for the next several days, will he? His horse and Usthius did the work, but he gets the credit! I'm glad I'm not a horse racer!" He howled with laughter and was joined wholeheartedly by Endemion, and hesitantly by both Usthius and me.

"It looks as if you had been in the games yourself, Bias," observed Endemion. "You did not compete today, did you? I didn't think you were interested in that sort of thing."

"Oh, I enjoy athletics well enough," I said. "But I'm not in the same league as you fellows. No, I was involved in a fire in the city of tents down by the shore of the Maeander. Have you heard about it?"

"Why, yes, word had reached us not long ago about a fire," Endemion said eagerly. "So you were in it, were you? Was anybody hurt? You don't look as if you fared any too well yourself!" His chest muscles rippled as he leaned toward me.

"At least four or five people were killed and some more injured," I replied softly. "I was with two who died. One was Polearchus of Miletus, the uncle of the athlete Habiliates."

"What ill fortune!" Mycrustes exclaimed. "First the nephew, then the uncle. That family should never have come here. They must have mightily offended some god." He took a large drink of wine

"Offended some god," I mused.

"Yes, indeed. Or some instrument of a god."

Endemion looked at me curiously for a moment, and then turned to Usthius. "Weren't you down there after the horse race, Usthius?" he asked. "After we cheered you on your victory and got back to the stadium, I remember you saying you had some business down by the Maeander and wouldn't be able to see us compete in the discus. You didn't mention that you saw the fire."

Usthius glanced sharply at Endemion, and answered offhandedly. "Yes, I was down near the city of tents, but my business was with a sheep merchant at the river's edge a little further to the east."

"So you never made it to the tent city?" I asked him with interest.

"I never intended to go to the tents," he replied, "and so I had no reason to 'make it there,' as you so quaintly put it. I never saw any fire, and didn't hear about it until I came here to the baths and overheard people talking about it."

He returned to drinking his wine. Both Mycrustes and Endemion looked at me with mild interest, but when I did not pursue the matter, turned back to a topic of unceasing concern to them: the competitions scheduled for tomorrow. Endemion was in a number of final events and was worried he would not be able to sustain himself for the pentathlon the next day, but Mycrustes, entered only in the discus final, encouraged him and soon had him chuckling and confident again. I remained for a few minutes more, watching Usthius, but finally decided to leave when he refused to meet my eyes but went on drinking. The other two athletes bade me a cheerful farewell, as I went from the cold room back into the changing area.

The slave had done a creditable job on my clothing, having washed away the worst of the blood and mud stains and then attempted to dry the garments by the huge hearth in the hot room. They were still damp to the touch, but I did not mind that and was grateful enough to reward the slave with a stater coin.

He took it without thanks and turned away to help another guest entering the room from the andron. Stifling a sudden spurt of anger that I realized had been caused by Usthius but would have been directed at this harmless servant, I hurried out of the baths and toward home.

Endemion's mention of Usthius' visit to the river set me to thinking anew. If I spoke to the various people involved in this situation so far, could they all account for their actions during the fire? If some of my suspects were not able to produce a witness to account for their whereabouts, that might help reduce the number of those who could have killed Polearchus and Machus. That is, of course, if the person who killed the Miletian and his servant was the same one who had murdered Tyrestes and Habiliates. Come to think of it, I thought, it is possible that they were not the intended victims, but that *I was*.

This thought was so startling that I stopped in my tracks, causing a visitor behind to collide with me. Muttering my apologies, I moved on down the street and out of Priene's western gate, grappling with this new idea.

Yes, suppose it was *I* the killer intended to stop? Perhaps he or she had seen me with Polearchus, overheard that I was going with him to his temporary home to talk about the mystery, and preceded us to the tent city. There the killer could have entered the tent, attacked Machus, and waited for us. If this was the case, then any of my suspects could be the Miletian's murderer!

But again, in that case, if one or more of them could not account for his actions during the fire, I could make some real progress in closing in on the killer. I wished that I had been able to recognize the shadowy intruder.

And then, the idea hit me. I am sure that Poseidon finally took pity on me and sent this consideration into my head.

The killer did not know that I could not identify him (or her?). It was possible that he or she didn't even know I was still alive. If I were a killer, would I have remained in the vicinity of the fire to be sure that my victims were really dead? It would be tempting, but dangerous. Suppose somebody saw him in the immediate area. How could he explain his way out of it? No, he would not have stayed. Too risky. Therefore, he would simply have hoped that nobody of any consequence saw him, and that all his intended victims were dead, no matter who they were.

If the killer did not know I was alive, he or she would be able to find out very shortly as news of the fire's victims spread through the city. But the murderer still would not know if I could identify him or her!

That was it then. The game was just about played out. I was in deadly danger all the time now. The murderer, having probably struck four times already, could not allow me to live. I had to bring the investigation to a close immediately, and reveal the murderer's identity, so that the magistrates and the victim's family could bring the culprit to justice. But I did not know who it was! How to do it? How?

Be calm, I told myself sternly. There must be a way. Just as I did not know the killer's identity, he or she conversely did not know how much I knew or if I could identify him. Poseidon, help me again, I begged silently. Agonizing moments stretched by.

Then suddenly, Poseidon revealed it to me! It would be extremely hazardous, but I was in mortal danger in any case. I had no time to check into the whereabouts of all the possible suspects in the case. I had no idea when the murderer might strike at me. Therefore, I had to gamble everything on one throw of the bones.

I had to set up a trap, and hope that it would be the killer and not I that would be caught in it.

Feverishly working out the details in my head, I turned up the path that led to the estate of Holicius and hurried home to eat a very late dorpon. I was suddenly ravenously hungry.

CHAPTER XXI

SETTING THE TRAP WAS not as difficult as I thought it would be.

After a restless night of tossing and turning on my cot, I dispatched Duryattes early in the morning to seek out Valato and ask the magistrate to contact the other "actors" in our little drama of death, and call them to a meeting in his house that evening. I would have chosen the daylight hours if I could, but since this was the day of many of the final athletic contests, nobody would have wanted to come! We Ionians love our sports, and even something as serious as murder would take second place to the great games.

The members of my family, as well as Duryattes, were shocked at my appearance when we gathered in the back garden for the ariston meal an hour after dawn. I think the time I had spent in the baths the night before had erased the worst of the ravages, but my calves were conspicuously pink and hairless, which my father and mother did not fail to notice. The pain in my head had receded to a dull ache, but I was careful to avoid touching the lump when I combed my hair. As for my ribs, I had Duryattes tightly wrap my torso in a long scarf before I put on my black tunic, so that injury was out of sight and only revealed itself in a wince or two, if I moved suddenly in the wrong direction.

Everyone hung on my words when I told them about the tent city fire, while I ate black olives and goat cheese. In order to keep my mother and the girls from worrying (not that they did not have good reason to worry), I did not mention the deaths of Polearchus and Machus in particular, nor did I tell them about my brush with the Fates in the blaze. My leg had been singed, I said, when I helped to fight the fire, and everybody thanked Poseidon profusely for my good luck in escaping worse injury. Tesessa looked at me thoughtfully when I gasped suddenly after I twisted about to fend off my youngest sister, who had tried to climb onto my lap. I smiled at my mother brightly to relieve her suspicions and was careful to behave normally while we all walked together to the stadium to enjoy the great events of the day.

To say that the athletics that day were an anticlimax for me is like saying that Helen of Troy was a fairly attractive woman. I watched them for form's sake, but my mind whirled this way and that, searching for the right things to say at tonight's meeting, while I stayed close to Holicius and kept a wary eye out for any attack. My father gratefully found a ready audience for his homilies about athletes, contests, culture, stadium architecture and a myriad of other subjects. I tried to keep Holicius and at least two or three of my sisters between Tesessa and me; she still looked at me suspiciously from time to time. My father had agreed to let the girls stay for today's events, so they could see the very best young men of the Ionian world, the kind of men they should wish for as future husbands. My sisters showed varying degrees of interest from little Elissa's total involvement with a little girl sitting next to her to Risalla's constant surveyance of the naked males.

The results of the contests were not as dramatic as the citizens of Priene could have wished. As Helios' chariot of the sun climbed in the morning sky and then passed overhead and began to descend in the west, our athletes did not perform as well as expected. We did well enough on the whole, but only first place in the games means anything. One could win any number of second or third places and still be disgraced.

Krelonan won the heavy wrestling event, as expected, throwing his final opponent, a monster from Teos, over his right shoulder to the great delight of the roaring crowd. And surprisingly, Mycrustes took the discus competition with an incredible toss that amazed even him, I think. His tremendous grin as he was presented with his crown of laurel leaves would have lit up a cavern on a stormy night.

Endemion's performance disappointed everybody. Although he pulled in several second places, he did not prevail in a single event. Recalling his comments in the baths the night before, I could only suppose that he was worried about participating in the pentathlon the next day and had not really put his heart into today's contests. Since the winner of the pentathlon was almost a god for a day, this attitude was understandable but not very satisfying for the home crowd, which grew louder and more scornful after every event as the day wore on. I noticed Endemion's father, Nolarion, scowling ferociously, as his son went down to defeat in contest after contest.

Duryattes rejoined us at midday, sidling up to me silently and scaring me half witless by tapping me on the shoulder from behind. After I cursed him roundly, he told me that Valato had agreed to the meeting and was summoning all concerned. A magistrate's summons did not have to be obeyed in our democratic city, but to ignore it was to cast immediate suspicion on yourself and your activities. They would certainly all be there.

The day ground away in excruciating slowness. After the last event, the javelin, ended and the crowd was dispersing through the stadium exits, I excused myself to Holicius and Tesessa. I had, I explained, some last minute business with the magistrates, and under my mother's anxious eye, set out with Duryattes for Valato's house. I had no intention of going anywhere alone that night, and described the situation and my plans to the boy as we strode along. His eyes grew wide with surprise and disbelief as we grew closer to the magistrate's mansion, and I believe that only his station as a servant kept him from calling me the biggest fool since Dionysus took his first innocent sip of wine. Nevertheless, he vowed manfully to remain at my side no matter what. Considering his size and stature, I took little comfort from that.

By the time we arrived at Valato's impressive estate, the principals had already gathered. They had obeyed the summons very promptly. Smothering a groan of apprehension, I was led into the large andron by one of Valato's servants, leaving Duryattes to fret alone at the portico's entrance. But even amidst the apprehension and worry, excitement was beginning to build in me, and I could feel my senses sharpening and my heart beating faster.

I entered the andron and conversation ceased. All eyes were turned on me in varying degrees of welcome, suspicion, or hostility. None of them, however, was indifferent. From left to right in a semi-circle they were all seated on chairs or reclining on couches, grapes, olives, or figs caught for just a twinkling of a moment between bowl and mouth. It was almost like a fresco, even to the detail of a silver cup raised in Euphemius' hand and frozen there for a fraction of a heartbeat. Then the movement and conversation returned, as I was grasped at the wrist by Valato, who had risen from his couch.

To my left in a pair of wing-footed chairs sat Nolarion and his son, engaged in an animated conversation about today's or tomorrow's contests; the magistrate had his hands curled around imaginary weights, and he was clearly instructing Endemion on how to get the most out of a long jump. Next to them reclined the storklike Euphemius with his glass of wine and his fingers caressing his iron gray beard. He and Usthius next to him were wearing their wreaths of laurel leaves, won during the horse race. Euphemius appeared languid and satisfied. Usthius, on the other hand, had visibly started when I appeared at the door, the wine in his glass sloshing over its edge to stain the hem of his white tunic. Next in the semi-circle was the gigantic Kreton, father of the seemingly innocent Bilassa. He was apparently bewildered about why he should be attending this meeting, and he glared about like an irritated bear awakened from a long winter's nap. He stared at me as I entered, and I cautioned myself that his gargantuan sons had undoubtedly told him about my conduct with his lusty little girl. Next to this aging Hercules sat the portly figure of my supposed superior, Crystheus, the major priest of the Panionian. I had wanted him here to confirm a portion of my plan, and it looked as if he were trying to be as ingratiatingly polite as he could to Kreton, who was snubbing him. Completing the circle on my immediate right was the couch of Valato, who was now guiding me by the elbow to a chair in the center of the semicircle. I thanked him as he resumed his place on his couch, but I was too nervous to sit and proceeded to pace about the inside of the andron, followed closely by seven pairs of eyes.

"Er . . . Bias," interjected Valato after a moment. "We are all here, as you have requested. I trust the object of our meeting is more important that watching you walk about the room?" He smiled slightly, and gestured for me to begin speaking. I gathered my wits about me, drawing them in as a fisherman would draw in his net.

"All of you are aware," I began, motioning particularly at Kreton and Usthius, "that I have been charged by Priene's magistrates to find the murderer of Tyrestes. To that end, I was presented with this warrant, authorizing me to speak to any citizen or slave about this matter." I waved the small piece of vellum in the air, and their eyes followed it.

"Since that time, several days ago, many things have happened. Let me tell you about them so that you will all know what wickedness has affected these games." I then related everything, starting with the deaths of Tyrestes and Habiliates and ending with the killing of Polearchus and his servant at the tent city.

I prudently omitted my conversations with Ossadia and Bilassa, noting Kreton seemed to become more bewildered at each word. Most of the guests knew about the deaths at the hippodrome already, but they appeared stunned to hear about the dead Miletians. I did not divulge my suspicions.

"Do you mean to say that there have been *three* guestslayings here during the games?" Crystheus wrung his hands as if to squeeze water out of them. "Three? Poseidon has surely shown his displeasure with our city in that case!"

"This is the first that I have heard of any of this," rumbled Kreton, peering angrily at me from beneath shaggy lowered brows. "What does this have to do with me? Why were you speaking to my daughter yesterday without my permission? It is impossible that she would have anything to do with this." He glared around the room like an infuriated bull, daring anybody to move. Careful, Bias, I cautioned myself, you are treading on very thin ice here.

"Noble Kreton, I apologize for speaking to your daughter without your approval," I said in what I hoped was an appropriately abject manner. "I misinterpreted the warrant given to me by the magistrates, and assumed it allowed me to act as I did. I certainly never intended to give offense to you or your innocent daughter."

The giant stared at me suspiciously for a moment, while some of the fire seemed to fade from his eyes. He glanced about the room, busied himself for a while straightening the folds of his voluminous chiton, and then spoke more calmly.

"Well, young man, your apology is accepted. Perhaps it is with the magistrates I need to speak about this warrant. On the other hand, that does not tell me *why* you felt you had to speak with her, in defiance of convention and my displeasure. What does she have to do with this evil business?"

"Sir, here was my reasoning. Bilassa knew Tyrestes was the new head of his family and saw that he wanted her to become mistress of his estate. You also knew this, and unless I am mistaken, allowed them to meet once so that

Tyrestes could talk to your daughter about it." Kreton regarded me with some surprise, and slowly nodded his massive head.

"Yes, that is so. I allowed them a time in our garden, but I didn't think that Tyrestes was favorably impressed, though only the gods know why. You have all seen my Bilassa. She would be a catch for any young man."

As long as he did not mind that she had bedded half the young men in Priene, I thought irreverently.

"As you say, noble Kreton," I agreed. "But you were mistaken in Tyrestes' intentions toward your daughter. He was most favorably impressed, and was simply waiting for the right moment to propose a betrothal agreement to you." The small lie rolled smoothly off my lips, and I sent a silent prayer to Aphrodite, the goddess of love, to forgive my transgression. "As such, I had hoped that your daughter, who is very intelligent, may have noted something about the young man that would have aided my investigation. Again, I know now that I overstepped the bounds of propriety, but my enthusiasm ran away with me, especially in the presence of your lovely little girl."

"Ah, indeed, so that was the way of it, eh?" he asked, in a much better humor. "And did you discover anything of substance from her?"

"No sir, I am afraid not." Simulated regret dripped from my words. "She was much too taken with the possibilities of life with Tyrestes to notice anything that might have helped me." I almost writhed with shame at this bald-faced lie, but I hoped that Poseidon wanted me to catch a guestslayer even at the cost of an untruth.

Kreton nodded massively, accepting this, and then Valato spoke.

"And I assume that is why you also spoke to my daughter, Ossadia?"

"Yes, sir," I answered quickly. "But in her case, she had become enamored from afar with the Miletian athlete Habiliates, and had no interest in Tyrestes. You yourself have witnessed what this innocent obsession has done to her. I was not able to obtain any relevant information from her either."

Valato's head bobbed up and down like a small bird's. "Quite so, quite so," he murmured swiftly. "But where does that leave you now, Bias?"

"Let us consider what we know here, sir," I said. "Why did each of these deaths take place? Murders are rare enough in our society that there must have been an overwhelming reason or urge for the killer to strike. Add in the miasma of guestslaying, and you have a man whose reason has been overpowered by one of the gods. This man is tainted forever in the sight of all gods and men. What could be his reasons for this incredible betrayal of his city and his religion?"

"Well, he must have had a personal vendetta against Tyrestes," ventured Nolarion. "Why else would he have hurt Priene's chances of winning the games? Tyrestes was the best athlete this city has produced since I won the pentathlon twenty years ago." Endemion glanced sharply at his father and then looked away, his face reddening in the glow of the late evening sunlight.

"Why indeed?" I echoed softly. "But what about the others? What about Habiliates?"

"Couldn't that have been an accident?" asked Euphemius with a shrug that set his storklike head bobbing and weaving. "I know that Polearchus felt that it was deliberate, but accidents do happen all the time in chariot racing and horse racing."

"No, I believe that Polearchus was correct, sir," I answered. "His master carpenter confirmed that the chariot axle had been sawed. Eliminating Habiliates would be an excellent step forward for someone to rank even higher in the games."

All eyes were on Endemion and Usthius with suspicion and distrust. Endemion was the first to protest.

"I will not be accused in this fashion," he shouted angrily as he leapt to his feet, followed swiftly by Euphemius' horseman, Usthius, who cried, "Nor I," his voice breaking like that of a youth balanced between boyhood and manhood. His fists clenched and unclenched, as he stared around the room.

"Nobody has accused you of anything," I said harshly. "There is still the matter of Polearchus and Machus." The two men glared fiercely about the andron, and then slowly perched on the edge of their chairs, like two birds on a branch.

"The matter of Polearchus and Machus," I repeated slowly. "What possible reason could there be for them to die? They were not competitors in the games." The room was silent, except for the ragged breathing of the two athletes. Then Valato cleared his throat.

"Polearchus had threatened to tell the citizens and the visitors about the guestslaying of Habiliates. Only the gods know what would have happened if he had done that."

"Would that have been enough reason?" I asked in a low tone. "I do not know. Is anybody concerned enough about Priene to kill for her in cold blood?"

"You have a lot of questions, and it appears that you have gathered precious few answers, Bias," said Nolarion. "If you know the identity of the murderer, tell us so that we may act." Two or three of the others nodded. I paused for several long moments before continuing.

"I believe that I may have the answer and your murderer. But I do not know for certain," I added.

"What else is there for you to do to find out?" asked Nolarion , his hands pulling angrily at his long beard. "How long will this go on?"

"It will be over by tomorrow," I said, looking about the andron in apparent satisfaction. The faces reflected incredulity, doubt, relief, and perhaps even envy. "I intend to go to the shrine of the god Poseidon tomorrow at dawn and ask for his guidance and wisdom. I feel that I am only a heartbeat away from the answer."

Heartbeat indeed, I thought . . . maybe my last one.

"A heartbeat away," repeated Kreton thoughtfully. "And you think Poseidon will provide you with an answer."

"He *is* a priest of Poseidon, you realize," spoke up a voice that had been almost unheard all evening. It was Crystheus, his face screwed up in what could only be described as holy indignation. He was speaking with uncanny accuracy, and I had not even asked! "The gods do favor their anointed with insights into the strange doings of man, do they not?" He stared belligerently around the room.

"Indeed they do, noble Crystheus," answered Nolarion shortly. "Indeed they do."

CHAPTER XXII

AND SO HERE I WAS. Hunched in the bowels of the sacred cave of Poseidon Helikonios, watching the murderer peering uncertainly into the gloom from the entrance, and trying to distinguish my form from the many statues that graced the cave floor. I saw his head lift expectantly, as I drew my father's old short sword across a bronze incense burner squatting next to me.

"Yes, I knew you would be here," he called softly. "The gods will not help you now, little priest. Your life has run its course, and this is the end of the race. You might as well accept your fate and come out. I promise that I will end it quickly and you will not have to suffer. That is a greater reward than many men receive at the end of their lives."

I drew a deep breath and replied, "I am not coming out, Guestslayer. But you may come in, and be cursed by Poseidon!" I saw the him grinning as he began to stalk slowly into the cavern, still unsure of my location in its dark interior. His sharp sword swished too and fro in front of him, as if testing the air for thickness.

"I am back here, Nolarion," I called out. "In the very back of this sacred ground. Are you going to compound your crimes by killing a priest of Poseidon on the god's own holy site?"

The grin remained plastered on the big magistrate's face like a fresco on a wall. He stopped about ten paces from me, peering closely and trying to distinguish me from the nearby statue of Cycnus, the son of Poseidon who had been slain by Achilles in the war against Troy. Since Cycnus had been invulnerable, the great Achilles had killed him by strangling him with his helmet strap. It flashed through my mind that at least I would not be killed in that fashion, since neither Nolarion nor I wore a helmet. Strange, some of the thoughts that assail one in times of danger. At any rate, I sidled a step closer to the statue to make it that much more difficult for Nolarion to find me.

"Oh, I don't think I have to worry about that, do I?" he protested with a chuckle. "After all, I have saved Priene from ruin by keeping the news of these guestslayings a secret. And when my son wins the pentathlon today, I think that Poseidon will certainly forgive any small transgressions I may have committed." He was still staring into the gloom, trying to distinguish me from the luckless Cycnus. Outside the sun was just breaking over the eastern horizon and throwing long shadows to the west from the several statues standing at the cave's entrance.

"Small transgressions?" I repeated incredulously. "You have killed four people, three of them guests in our city! Surely you realize that because of this evil your shade will find no rest."

"I think we will let the gods decide that," he said mildly. "I believe that when the time comes for my spirit to pass to the underworld, the god Hades will understand and sympathize with me." He stooped to strike the ground with his unencumbered hand out of respect for the lord of the underworld.

"Why did you do it? Why did you kill them all? How can you justify the murders of the city's champion athlete and three guests at the games?" I needed to have him confess his crimes out loud, to confirm my suspicions. He stopped for a moment and looked cautiously around him. Then he turned his attention back to me and my marble companion.

"You mean you do not know why I killed them?" he inquired in a puzzled tone. "You really do not know? I knew you were no sophist, Bias, traveling from city to city spreading your wisdom, but I did not realize you were a complete idiot." He smiled complacently and stepped a pace nearer to me.

"Obviously Tyrestes had to die, so that his efforts would not distract Endemion from winning his events. My son was the better athlete, of course, but he needed to compete against the visitors from the other Ionian cities, not against a citizen of our own fair Priene. After all, it is his fate to carry on the glory that I obtained for the city twenty years ago at the same games. Tyrestes had no such legacy to fulfill and might have kept my boy from achieving his destiny. I obviously could not allow that to happen."

"But if Endemion was the better athlete, then he would have won against Tyrestes anyway!" I objected, hoping to keep the magistrate talking as long as possible.

"Bias, you know as well as I do that the gods will always play their little games." He waved his sword about to emphasize his words. "There is no telling what they may have come up with if I had not balanced the scales." He took another step forward.

"And Habiliates?" I asked. "Was it necessary to balance the scales there as well?"

"Of course it was," he said. "He was much too good a runner to be allowed to continue competing. Just think how it would have delighted the gods to keep my son from winning by favoring an athlete from Miletus! Even you, Bias, have to admit that Miletus has more than enough power and glory already. Certainly, we do not need to supply them with more! It is hard enough keeping our independence here in Priene as it is. As a magistrate, I can tell you that Miletus is constantly encroaching upon our city's territorial prerogatives and trade routes. We have enough to contend with in holding the empire of Lydia at bay on our eastern borders. Let me tell you, young man, it is not easy to compete every day with the greatest city in the Greek world."

It was difficult to believe that this murdering hound was lecturing me on politics, but there it was. Anything to keep him talking.

"How did you manage to damage his chariot without being seen?" I inquired curiously. "Surely there were citizens about who saw you working on that axle?"

"Not at all. I did my work in the hours of darkness. None of the horses or chariots are guarded at night, you know. It was a matter of only a few moments' work. Who would ever tamper with a chariot or animal destined to compete in the games the next day? Our security in such matters in woefully lacking. I really must speak to my fellow magistrates about that." He appeared to be making a mental note in his head.

"And so that brings us to Polearchus and Machus," I concluded. "Did you kill them because they were Miletians too?"

"No, of course not! Well, perhaps partially," he confessed. He was only about six paces from me now and presumably could distinguish me from the statue of Cycnus. "Miletus is much too powerful a state to insult and turn to a wrathful enemy. I must admit it was hard on my conscience at first to kill Tyrestes. It was hard but necessary. But the Miletian and his slave? That was enjoyable! But, naturally, the real reason they had to die was that they were going to announce the guestslaying of Habiliates to all the crowds! Surely you can see that would have been disastrous. I hope I am a better magistrate than to allow such a catastrophe as that to happen to my home city!"

"But you are the one who caused the problem in the first place," I pointed out in an exasperated tone. "If you had not killed Habiliates, they would not have had anything to tell the people!"

"Yes, I suppose that is true enough. But the charioteer was killed for an entirely different reason. He had to be removed in order to eliminate Miletian competition. Why, Polearchus and that slave were being hardheaded and unreasonable! Could I allow Priene to be injured by their unreasonable attitude? Remember, Bias, moderation in all things is a virtue. We must not allow ourselves to become so embroiled in a matter that we lose our sense of moderation, as Polearchus did."

Moderation in all things! It was crystal clear now that the gods had robbed Nolarion of his sense of moderation, and indeed, of his mind as well. But there was still one last thread to be pulled.

"And me?" I asked quietly. "Why was it necessary to kill me? I did not know that you were the murderer at that time." He looked at me in bewilderment for a moment.

"I am sorry about that, you know," he replied. "I did not wish to injure you or cause you pain. But it was clear that you were drawing too close to the answers. And besides, what else could I do at the time? You were right there with the Miletian! How could I eliminate him without your seeing everything? And you may have recognized me anyway! Really, Bias, that was a ridiculous question." He took one more slow step towards me and grinned again.

"But enough conversation!" he said happily. "Do you wish for your death to be quick or will you make the pretense of fighting me?" He hefted his sword as if it were a light twig in his hand and stepped forward to begin a swing. My grip tightened on my own weapon, and my legs bunched in readiness for his attack.

"I do not think he will receive either," boomed a voice from behind us. Nolarion whirled with an exclamation in time to see four huge figures emerge from niches in the cave wall, two from our right and two from the left. Swords gleamed in the hands of three of them, and a spear was balanced by Krelonan the wrestler.

"Bias asked us after the meeting last night to conceal ourselves this morning in these statue niches," announced Kreton, gesturing at himself and his three Herculean sons, who strode up next to him to form an impassable barrier across the mouth of the cave. "He told me he had the murderer narrowed down to one of several people, and that he had made his announcement of plans in order to set a trap for the swine. We have been waiting here for hours in the hopes of snaring our quarry, and by Artemis the huntress, it appears that we have succeeded! We heard everything you said, Magistrate."

Nolarion swung his leonine head back and forth between the four big men, silently sizing them up.

"This is not your quarrel nor your business," he protested. "You are a worldly man, Kreton. Surely you can see that my actions were necessary. Your presence is not needed here."

The giant aristocrat shook his head grimly.

"You are a guestslayer and have disgraced our city," he snarled. "You must stand before the families of Tyrestes and Habiliates at the Podium of Justice and confess your crimes." Nolarion stared at the four huge men. Yes, I suppose I must," he mused after a few moments. "But first, let me conclude my business here!"

He threw a gracious smile at Kreton, whirled suddenly, and lunged at me with his short sword! I flung myself desperately backwards, simultaneously throwing my own sword up to deflect his blow. His blade clanged off the arm of the demi-god Cycnus, knocking out a sizable chunk of stone bicep, and he pulled it back to try for another blow. I was still off balance and twisted to my left to try and escape. His sword began its descent, slowly, and I knew I could not block it in time.

Then he simply stopped. His whole body jerked violently as if some puppeteer were tugging on his limb strings, and he stared dumbfounded down at his chest. Protruding from the front of his torso and parting his beard neatly in the middle was the point of a spear! He glared at it in wonder as the front of his chiton quickly turned bright red, touched it tentatively with a gnarled finger, dropped his weapon from his other hand, and very slowly turned to face Kreton again. The haft of the spear, jutting out of his back, swung around with him like some strange new appendage.

"I do not think . . ." he started to say, but was cut off when a gush of bright blood erupted from his mouth and ran down his chin. He coughed once, his legs giving way beneath him, and sagged to the cave floor. The point of the spear caught in the ground as he fell, and he lay there, supported by it in a triangular shape. The statue of Cycnus looked down on him stonily, nettled no doubt by the missing hunk of his arm. I stood, breathing in rasping whoops, my sword hanging uselessly by my side. The four big men walked slowly up to the body.

"Why, by the gods, boy, did you have to hit him in the chest?" Kreton asked Krelonan in exasperation. "Now there will be precious little satisfaction for the families of Tyrestes or Habiliates!"

"I am sorry, Father," replied the embarrassed wrestler. "You know I'm not accurate with the javelin. That is why I didn't compete in that event."

CHAPTER XXIII

VERY FEW PEOPLE KNEW about the crimes of Nolarion. And if those few had anything to say about it, which they did, no one else would ever find out. At least that was the hope—it may have been a vain one, of course, since conversation flowed like water between the privileged classes of the various city-states of Ionia.

Did I mention that the Ionian love of sport and spectacle exceeded our regard for almost everything else in our world? In any case, we were back at the stadium by midmorning. Kreton and his three gigantic offspring, after lugging the murderer's body secretly to the house of Valato, had set off for the athletic area to find Bilassa and her maid. I had stayed for an hour at the small magistrate's house, explaining the entire situation, and asking for further instructions. Valato had cautiously approved my actions, although some of them seemed to have surprised him. He instructed me not to tell anybody of the death of Nolarion until the games were concluded—especially not Endemion, who was Priene's last best chance for the pentathlon victory. Haven't I said that we were mad about sport?

I entered the stadium through a tunnel and found my family in their reserved seats, the girls sandwiched between my mother and father. Ulania's young man was there, under the watchful eye of my father, whose compressed lips and narrowed eyes betrayed his disapproval of this unconventional behavior. I supposed he tolerated it only because Ulania, though pleasant enough, was not in great demand and he had six daughters to marry off.

The competition for the long jump was almost completed. A muscular competitor from Phocae was making his third and last try. Grasping a jumping weight in each hand, he was trying to coordinate the swing of the weights with his hop, step, and jump. He curved off to the right in the last jump and only achieved twelve lengths of the fifteen he would have needed to win. The pentathlon would be won only by the first competitor to accomplish three clear victories in the five events: the long jump, discus, javelin, sprinting, and wrestling.

An athlete from Chios made a tremendous leap on his first try, fully fifteen lengths, to the earsplitting roar of approval from the crowd. The noise made conversation impossible, at least with my family. But I was sought out by others who thirsted for details of my investigation.

The magistrate Euphemius sought me out first, drawing me away from the discus competition. He asked me whether I had known at the gathering the night before, whether Nolarion was the Guestslayer.

"Well, sir, I had narrowed down the possible suspects as I went along, and he was the most logical choice. You see, as more people were murdered, the choice of murderer narrowed accordingly. Any of my original suspects could have killed Tyrestes. Habiliates' death lessened the choices, but my interviews with several of the suspects led me to drop them as possible killers." I hurried on, not wanting to mention the names of Ossadia or Bilassa.

"When Polearchus and his carpenter were slain in the tent city, it was clear that Nolarion had the most to gain or lose in this dangerous game. Endemion had no reason to kill the Miletians and neither had Usthius, though both had reason to slay Tyrestes and Habiliates."

"And what about Kreton," Euphemius asked, trying to keep one eye on me and one on the discus thrower on the stadium floor below. "Why was he at the meeting last night?"

"His daughter, Bilassa, had given me valuable information about Tyrestes and Usthius," I explained warily, to avoid falling into the rushing stream of lies, as I crossed wet stones of fact. "I felt that he deserved to attend because of that, and I needed the help of him and his sons to capture the killer at dawn."

Euphemius' attention returned wholly to me, and it was several moments before he spoke.

"And me, young Bias?" he asked very softly. "How did you know I was not your killer? You suspected me with the rest, of course." I stared at him in surprise and some little admiration.

"Yes, sir, I did suspect you with the others. But while you had reason to eliminate Habiliates, so that you could win the chariot race, and Polearchus, in order to save the city from damage and embarrassment, you had no reason to kill Tyrestes. You had no daughters to protect, and no sons to promote."

When the tall, stork-like magistrate glanced sharply at me, I realized I shouldn't have mentioned daughters.

"So I eliminated you as a suspect, just as I eliminated your driver, Usthius," I stammered quickly. "But for different reasons, of course."

He continued to look at me, and I began to sweat beneath my black tunic. If word of my knowledge of the innocent dallyings of Ossadia or the not-so-innocent dallyings of Bilassa ever got back to Valato or Kreton, my career in the priesthood of Poseidon could be brought to an abrupt halt. Not that it was the greatest career in the world so far, but one has to start somewhere.

"I think I understand, Bias," Euphemius said slowly. "You have done remarkably well. I won't forget your success or the dangers that you faced to arrive at the truth." He stopped and stared into my eyes. "The truth is very important, you know. It has to be tempered in the forge of expedience, of course, but it cannot be disregarded."

"No, sir, I agree with you completely." I sighed with relief.

"At any rate, let us go enjoy the games! Although I would hate to be the one to tell young Endemion about his father's crimes and fate, eh?"

"Begging your pardon, sir, you or the magistrate Valato will have to be the one to tell him. There is nobody else of sufficient rank and stature."

"You're right," he answered after a long pause. "I will talk to Valato and decide how to handle this tonight."

The competition proceeded through the morning and into the late afternoon with no clear pentathlon winner. The Chiosian athlete had won the long jump, and a boy from Colophon took the discus. Our own Mycrustes gave his all in the latter contest, but wasn't able to come anywhere close to his previous day's throw.

The excitement grew as the competition went on. Endemion's showing in the jump and the discus was respectable and nothing more. The home crowd began to grow restless after his performance in the discus, but he redeemed himself with a magnificent javelin toss on his second try, securing that victory for himself.

I was sitting with my family, next to my mother, when the sprinting event was scheduled to commence. Elissa climbed onto my lap, and drifted off to sleep with her golden head against my shoulder. Tesessa and I exchanged smiles; I knew she would not smile when she heard what had happened that morning.

My father's surprise announcement came at almost the same time that the competitor for Colophon won the sprint by just beating out Endemion. Holicius had been talking animatedly to the father of Ulania's betrothed between the running heats.

"That is settled then!" he announced triumphantly. Seated next to him, Mesivicus, the short, plump father of the spotty betrothed young man, beamed broadly.

"Mesivicus and I have decided that Albiades and Ulania will be wed in the month of Pyanopsion, just after the festival of Apaturia," Holicius continued. "That is just about five months away, and will give us plenty of time for planning the dowry and celebration!" My sisters squealed, bouncing excitedly on the seats, my mother smiled warmly at the news, and the betrothed pair at the end of the row blushed and looked everywhere but at each other. Well, that is good news, I thought. It is comforting to have good news on such a day.

The wrestling event was next in the competition. Various athletes were thrown this way and that until only two were left, Endemion and an unlikely looking specimen from Lebedos. The unlikely looking specimen was quite proficient, however, and the afternoon was waning when Endemion suddenly got the upper hand, twisted the Lebedoian's left arm behind him, and shoved his face into the ground for the win. The stands went wild, the delirious cheers rebounding from the walls.

The five events were complete, and there was no clear winner of three of them. The Colophonian had captured the discus and running competitions, the Chiosian the long jump, and Endemion the javelin and wrestling. So the struggle for the pentathlon crown was between those three. Each would keep the victory in his event until ousted by one of the other two, so that eventually one of them would emerge triumphant. I have to admit that the excitement was catching, and I cheered as lustily as the rest for our own competitor. Now, it would really be a matter of who tired first.

The long jump was held again, the three superb athletes leaping as far as possible, holding the jumping weights. Again, the Chiosian won easily, and stayed in the competition. The discus and javelin events proved to be the same, with the former winners again emerging triumphant. The mood of the spectators bordered on hysteria, with waves of emotion crashing back and forth between the sides of the stadium like tides on a rocky shore. The noise was deafening, and as the three men assumed their places for the sprint, it reached a crescendo. My three youngest sisters clapped their hands over their ears, and I sat on the edge of my marble seat in anticipation of Endemion's victory. The sprint had been won before by the Colophonian, but not by more than a half-length.

The runners crouched at the starting line, their toes bunched against the marble starting blocks. The judge dropped the starting cloth, and the whole thing became an anticlimax. Endemion slipped as he got off to a bad start, and the Colophonian shot out like an arrow to an easy victory.

So now it was down to the wrestling again. The three athletes drew lots to see who would wrestle first, leaving the third man with the advantage of being fresh for the final match. Either Endemion or the Chiosian had to win this event for the competition to revolve again to another round of the long jump. The judges conferred quietly for a moment, their bearded faces pressed close together to hear each other in the noisy crowd, and then announced that the wrestling would be confined to one fall only. This raised the crowd's emotion another notch.

The Colophonian drew the winning lot, so he sat tensely at the sidelines while Chiosian and Prienian circled each other before grappling. They strained back and forth mightily for a moment, and then the Chiosian was falling backwards, his arms revolving wildly. As good as he was in the long jump, he really was not much of a wrestler.

That left Endemion and the Colophonian. After a quick swig of cold water, they were in the center of the wrestling area. Endemion was the faster of the two, moving like an eel from the Aegean Sea, and leaped to grasp his opponent's left arm, twisting it behind the man to elicit a howl of pain.

They danced a strange duet for a heartbeat as the Colophonian strove to rid himself of the Prienian's hold, and Endemion forced his opponent's left arm behind his head.

The Colophonian broke free, holding his left arm close to his side, obviously to keep it from further injury. His face twisted in agony. Was the arm broken? Certainly many bones had been smashed in the wrestling events before now. Endemion's wolflike grin reminded me grimly of the look on his father's face, as he closed swiftly with the injured man.

Then, suddenly, it was over. The Colophonian's good right hand shot out, seized Endemion by the throat forcefully while his supposedly damaged left hand darted down to close onto the Prienian's right thigh muscle. A mighty heave and Endemion was on his knees, clutching his aching throat with both hands as the Colophonian raised his arms in triumph! A prodigious howl of disappointment erupted from most of the crowd, but the judges were already at the Colophonian's side, supporting his upraised arms to show that he was declared the pentathlon winner.

The crowd streamed out of the stadium, some headed for various taverns in the town, some for the tent cities, some for the baths, some for home. The religious ones, and most of the athletes, wended their way back over the spine of Mount Mycale toward the Panionion. At the sacred site of Poseidon Helikonios the victor would be officially crowned, and sacrifices would be offered by the chief priest Crystheus.

Tesessa and the girls began the long walk home, accompanied by Duryattes and Dryses. Holicius and I set out over the mountain to the altar site. Halfway there we were overtaken by Kreton and his three sons, all happily inebriated. The giant aristocrat proceeded to fill my father in on my adventures in the cave of Poseidon. He was quite an accomplished storyteller, and as all good storytellers will do, took the opportunity to embellish the exploits both of me and his Herculean children.

"Is all this true, then, Bias?" asked Holicius, when he managed to get a word in. "Nolarion was the murderer and is now dead? Does Endemion know?"

"Of course, it is true, noble Holicius," bellowed Kreton, flinging a gigantic friendly arm around my father's shoulders. "My son, Krelonan, skewered him like a lamb chop on a spit. And as for Endemion, who knows if he knows? The damned rascal lost the pentathlon for us, so who cares? The other two magistrates will tell him about his father's treason." Who, indeed, would care about a young man who tried his very best, but was not quite good enough, I reflected wryly. His own father had seen the truth long ago, I supposed.

My father suffered in the strong embrace of the big man.

"Why didn't you tell me about these dangerous exploits, my son?" wheezed Holicius, when he was able to catch his breath.

"He was probably just too modest," Kreton roared. "He was brave, very brave, and cunning too. It was well done, very well done!" He stopped abruptly and looked at my father and me.

"He has met my Bilassa, you know," he said in a thunderous whisper, scratching his tangled beard with his free hand as he continued to hold Holicius prisoner. "My beautiful, modest Bilassa. Say, isn't Bias your heir and not yet betrothed?" Staring up at the giant aristocrat, my father's small face was split by a smile that stretched from ear to ear.